Conversation
with a Killer

DeShawn Kenner

ISBN: 0989785424
ISBN-13: 978-0989785426

Layout by Sarah Anne Hubbard
Cover Design by Okamoto Studios

Kenner Publishing
Lindenhurst, NY

Printed in the U.S.A.

Dedication

This book is dedicated to everyone who has gone down the wrong path, it is never too late to switch to the right path. Also, to everyone who passes judgment on those, remember we are all one circumstance away from taking the wrong path.

Acknowledgments

Hats off to programs such as Rising Hope and Hudson Link for providing men and women whom are incarcerated the opportunity to get degrees, and therefore change the trajectory of their lives permanently. Recidivism rates prove the importance of programs such as these.

Thank you to Mercy College and Columbia University for providing their Professors and courses offered to take place in some NYS prisons. These educational institutions represent the best of humanity, because they are helping to create the positive role models and leaders that our society so desperately needs.

Contents

Disclaimer

This is a work of fiction. Names, characters, businesses, places, events, and incidents are either the products of the author's imagination or used in a fictitious manner. Any resemblance to actual persons, living or dead, or actual events is purely coincidental.

DeShawn Kenner

Introduction

The objective of this book is to analyze and possibly discover why I turned to crime and murder. As a child I had dreams of growing up to be a lawyer, doctor, or scientist; however, it did not turn out that way. Ultimately, I was sentenced to life in prison, or I would be so old when I got out, that I would wish I were dead.

Where had it all gone wrong for me? Why had I picked up those guns? Why had I sold those drugs? Why had I robbed people? Overall, why had I become a dangerous threat to the civilized world? Had I even seen myself as a threat?

I am going to reflect on my family, my community, my conditions, and most importantly myself. I'm going to be as honest as I can possibly be not only to the reader but also to myself.

After all this will be a mission for the truth behind my actions. My soul hopes and prays that something positive will be discovered in the process of my mental and spiritual investigation. Let us begin...

DeShawn Kenner

Part One:

Upbringing

DeShawn Kenner

Mother

I was birthed by a teenage mother who was in foster care at the time, no more than seventeen years old. She had been in foster care since she was 5 years old. She was taken by child protective services, from her mother whom was an alcoholic and deemed unfit to care for her only child. My mother not only had no siblings, she did not have any close relatives either. She never knew her father in any way. Her mother did not know who he was or at least she never revealed it to my mother. My mother's mother left Baton Rouge Louisiana while still pregnant with my mother, relocated to New York leaving behind everybody and everything she had known, for reasons still a mystery to me.

My mother Charlotte had three children by three different men by the time she was 22 years old. By Charlotte, I have a sister 14 months younger and a brother five years younger than myself. My sister's name is Shawnika and my brother's name is Lincoln. Charlotte was a high school dropout and a very attractive young girl who lived in poverty. She had light brown skin, long hair, a pretty face, and a super curvy figure; even after having all three of her kids.

I remember as a little boy I would walk behind my mother as we strolled down the street to block the view of her butt, because so many guys would be checking her out as we passed. During that time, I was a mama's boy who hated any guy looking at her with hungry eyes. My mother and father were never a couple, they just created me. I'll get to my father next. Charlotte was with my sister's father and brother's father for short periods of time, both were abusive relationships for her. She was in a few abusively violent relationships; one situation stands out in my mind. A guy she was with beat her viciously right in front of me with closed fist punches fit for a man. I was no more than 5 or 6 years old, I was terrified of him. My mom told me to go get help, but he forcefully told me I better not move. I just stood there frozen with fear. She survived the assault then we walked to the hospital to get her some medical attention. Even as a kid I now realize that fear can turn into rage. After that incident I swore to myself that I would kill him or anybody else that hurt my mother like that again. I could not wait to grow up, I would be the protector of my family. I was the oldest; my mom, sister, brother, and I were all that we had in this world. Like it or not I had to get tough and be tough.

In hindsight I can see that my mom was a kid raising kids, with no biological family around to help support or guide her choices; and she had no high school diploma, GED, or vocational trade certification. In the words of Langston

Hughes, it was "A Dream Deferred." As a young girl I don't know what Charlotte's plan was, or if she even had a plan at all. It must have been rough and uncomfortable growing up in foster care and group homes, constantly surrounded by strangers. What she was going through or what was on her mind could only be explained by her.

Despite Charlotte's situation, whether her problems were karma, self-inflicted, or both; she never abandoned us, she was the best mother she knew how to be. We were learning and growing up with her. She settled in Mount Vernon, New York which borders the Bronx, Yonkers, and Pelham. She more than likely settled there because all three of her baby daddies lived out there, it was the last place she was in school, and one of the last places she was in foster care. She had grown fond of the foster family she lived with out there. They were a Black, deeply religious Christian family of four. A father, mother, son, and daughter; they were members of a local church. My mother also at some point became a member. That family may have helped to cultivate her belief in God. Charlotte passed on her love for God to us. We even went to the same church as kids most Sundays. She taught me the Lord's Prayer and the 23rd Psalm, which for the most part I still know. Although Charlotte frequented church she was still in the streets. She could have been considered a fast-young girl at that time. She had 3 kids, no real man in her life, she used drugs, drank alcohol, smoked cigarettes, and partied; all while making sure all our needs were met. I know she loved us, we were some spoiled poor kids. I say that because even though she had no real job or real source of income, anything we asked her for she got it for us, by any means necessary.

She kept us dressed to impress, well fed, in a clean nice apartment, and with more toys than

Toys R Us. Charlotte made efforts to get her life together for the greater good of us and herself. She earned her GED. She went to hair school for a while but did not complete her licensing for whatever reasons. She ended up getting her CDL driver's license and was hired to drive school buses in Mount Vernon. She met and married a man named Big Bo. He was good to her and us for the most part. He had done at least 10 years up north in New York State prison for armed robbery. He was diesel, he had muscles everywhere. He was well-kept, had crooked teeth, and was a coffee colored fellow with waves in his hair. While up north he learned how to paint, and when he came home that was how he made his living, how he supported us all.

I do not know where or when my mother met Big Bo. One summer after Shawnika and I returned from vacation in California and got back to our tiny 2-bedroom apartment on the third floor was when we first met Bo. He was sitting on the windowsill with a blue du-rag on his head, a Gold's Gym tank top, some blue jeans, and boots with a gold chain around his neck. He did not say anything, and we did not either, that was in 1986.

There was no wedding when Bo and my mom got married; Shawnika, Lincoln, nor I even knew. They slipped off and did it on the low. I did not really care for Big Bo or any other man that my mother had been with, but he was there and as a kid under my mom's roof I had to deal with it. He took on the role of provider, protector, and punisher of us three children. As the punisher he gave out disciplinary consequences. My mother's and his two main forms of punishment were to keep us in our room, no going outside to play; or to beat us with a heavy hand, a heavy belt, or a heavy switch. I was never all right with it; especially when I had to take my clothes off for a whipping. Charlotte and Bo got along well from what I could tell. He beat us kids but never beat her. He became my mom's enforcer; that was a change for her. Her ex-lovers would beat her and not us, but this one beat us and not her.

There was one other guy that I can think of who my mother was with that put hands on me aggressively and violently. His name was Devan he had beady eyes, pitch black skin with a short nappy afro, and two missing front teeth. He wore a lot of gold on his hands, neck, and wrists; and he had a heavy accent. I could barely understand him. I do not know what she saw in him. He was not easy on the eyes, for Charlotte to be so beautiful she had strange taste in men. They were never tall, attractive, educated, or well-to-do; which includes my own father. I love him, but I must be honest. She always chose older men, they never seemed like the type, I would imagine her with.

With Bo it was not all bad. He introduced us to his mother, father, and brother; they were nice people. His family had a boat that looked like a baby yacht to me. It had an upstairs, downstairs, beds, kitchen, bar, bathroom, fishing rods on the deck, and all that good stuff. Their boat was always docked and ready to ride. They invited us on fishing trips. They fished for Porgies way out in the Atlantic Ocean. They bought us kids small fishing rods, it was the first time I had ever caught a fish. It tugged on the line and the rod bent over, Bo's father Ben told me to reel it in. I unlocked the reel and began winding it. I felt like I was playing tug-of-war with a great sea monster. When it finally emerged from the water it was hard for me to believe that the warrior on the hook was just a small spotted fish about 4 inches long. The fish was bucking like a bull with a cowboy on its back. Ben grabbed it firmly by the body took the hook out of its jaw, let us kids look at it, then tossed it back into the ocean. It was some sort of a Crappie. He said we only wanted Porgies, a thicker meatier fish. Overall it was a great time. I wondered to myself after that, why did Bo commit robbery if he had this great support of family?

Bo and Charlotte would take us on road trips just to get out of the hood for a while. Great Adventure, Dorney Park, Kings Dominion, were just some of the entertaining fun places we went to in that old Chevy wagon. Those were good times. It was important to her that her three children experienced things outside of the poor neighborhood we lived in. At first just Shawnika and I, then Lincoln too would go out to California to stay with Shawnika's biological grandfather in Oakland for summer vacation for most of the 1980s. I grew up with her father and his family too, they had known me since I was a baby. They embraced me, treated me, and made me feel like one of their own. Black, my sister's father and Charlotte were constantly fighting. I mean physically fighting not just arguing. It was bad, but nothing compared to Ice, my brother's father was a beast.

No man that Charlotte had been with compared to Ice when it came to being crazy. He sold drugs, was shooting heroin, drank liquor, and beer, rolled himself and me joints of weed up in Ez-Wider, kicked my mother around like a soccer ball, and kept a pistol. He was a Savage. Remember when I said I was frozen in fear while Charlotte was being brutalized? It was Ice. I am surprised Charlotte could even love a man after what she experienced with her three children's fathers. My father may not have beat her, but he was nowhere to be found either.

Ice got so out of control with beating Charlotte that she got in contact with her biological mother's nephew Lindsey. He was a country boy from down in Louisiana. Although Charlotte had been taken from her mother, they managed to keep some level of contact, their love did not die. Nor did the love between cousins, because when Charlotte called, Lindsey came to do something to Ice. It was dark outside when Lindsey arrived, he showed up with two of his comrades. They all had assault rifles out, like it was legal. Charlotte had to know they were coming because we were outside waiting for them. Ice was barricaded upstairs in the small apartment. They were getting ready to go up there and get him. I felt relieved and could not wait. I just kept looking up to the third-floor window that Ice was behind. Lindsey and his two soldiers were dead serious about their mission, but Charlotte panicked, it was too real for her to handle. She started screaming at the top of her lungs and shouting, "no don't do it!" She jumped in front of them blocking their path upstairs, she was drawing attention to the situation, and made it hot for them. Lindsey was pissed, he told my mother to never call him again, and then vanished with his team before someone called the cops. I was mad at her, why didn't she let it go down? I knew that he deserved whatever they had planned for him. I wanted to see him come through that window, I was staring up at. A part of me thought Ice would go out like an OG blasting, but nope he hid up in that apartment like a fox from the hounds. We did not go back upstairs that night; we went to a neighbor's house. When we returned the following day he was gone, I never saw him again. Bo was the next man to move into the tiny apartment with us, that apartment saw more action than the soldiers in Iraq.

Next to my mother, Shawnika was my first best friend, we went through those challenges together. Lincoln was too little to remember Ice or those soggy sad times. The only father he ever knew was Bo. I was very protective of Lincoln; he was my brother. Bo and Charlotte had promise between them. Both worked, did the right thing, and took us to church. We almost made it up out of that small two-bedroom apartment. Bo and Charlotte shared a bedroom; Shawnika, Lincoln, and I shared the other. Lincoln wet his bed which left a slight stench of urine in the air, it drove me crazy. What stopped Bo and Charlotte's progressive campaign to get us out of the hood? I will explain shortly.

Although Charlotte and her mother had reconnected, they still had mother daughter issues. Charlotte and her mother were in love at the same time. Charlotte and Bo, her mom Betty Jo and Peter. Betty Jo wanted them all to be married on the same day as part of one ceremony, but Charlotte was not with it. They had a falling out and stopped speaking for almost two years.

Betty Jo and Peter would come down to visit us in our small apartment 3C. We had a roach infestation in that place. One evening Betty Jo, Peter, Charlotte, Bo, and the rest of us were sitting in the living room watching some movie on the television, when two roaches decided to trap themselves between the glass and screen of the television set. They became part of the movie; nobody could get them out. That apartment had to be roach bombed once every two weeks. We were running through more roach spray than a busy taxi cab did gas per day. We had a cat that used to eat the roaches, along with any mice he could find.

In comparison Betty Jo had a beautiful home up in Peekskill New York. The air was fresher, the neighborhood was spotless and quiet. Betty Jo was a tall, slender, cocoa complexioned woman, with jet black thick long hair, high cheekbones, and a heavy southern drawl. She cussed like a sailor with the attitude to match. Shawnika and I got a kick out of listening to her go off while she was driving. She would be cursing the other motorists out, while speeding past them.

I had grown chubby one summer out in California and couldn't shake the weight off. Betty Jo told me that if I got any fatter, she would have to make me some pants out of potato sacks. That was what all the little fat boys had their clothes made from when she was growing up, because they could not fit in anything else. Despite her message she always had at least two cakes and a large crystal bowl filled with every type of chocolate candy imaginable for us to enjoy.

My grandmother whipped my butt twice. The first time was because I stashed all those chocolate candy wrappers underneath the cushions of her gorgeous couch which had a plastic cover over it. Why did I do it? I was being sneaky not wanting her to find out that I was eating all the candy. After that spanking, she told me not to ever do that again because I didn't have to hide anything from her, we were family, and she bought the candy for us to enjoy. The second beating was much more severe. Betty Jo had a brown paper bag on top of a tall dresser in her room that she instructed me never to touch. I wanted to see what was in that bag, I had to know. One day she went down into the basement to wash a load of laundry. When I was sure she was all the way down in the laundry room part of the basement, I hurried to her room. I was not tall enough to reach the bag, so I stepped into a laundry basket filled with clothes which was on the side of the dresser, closest to the brown paper bag. I reached up and grabbed the bottom of the bag, it was so heavy I had to pull harder on it. With the help of my hand the weighted bag left the top of the dresser, flew right past me, and landed on soft plush light brown carpet. Something had ripped through the bag and was protruding out of the side of it. I stepped out of the basket and swooped down on the bag. I unrolled the top of it and saw the handle of the gun. As I pulled out the gun by the wooden handle, the nose of the big black revolver tore through the side of the bag. At the exact same time Betty Jo walked back into her room for that other basket of laundry, I was just standing in. In that very moment when I turned and saw her coming in; I could have crapped on myself and then threw up at the same time. I was caught red-handed with no excuse. She grabbed the gun and the torn bag and placed them on the bed. She then snatched me up off the floor fast and pinned me to her body with one of her arms,

I felt like I was in a vice grip. Then she slapped me what seemed like a hundred times until I was screaming with tears. That was my fee for being curious and hardheaded. Over the next few years I was compliant to all her rules and regulations. She had tamed me with the power of corporal punishment. Indirectly at the same time she taught me the power of it.

Sadly, Betty Jo was diagnosed with brain cancer. We spent her last days with her at her house. She grew baseball sized lumps on her head. She lost all her hair. She smoked cigarettes before she was diagnosed and already was suffering from chronic emphysema, which made it very difficult for her to breathe. She had all types of tubes plugged into her beautiful dark, now frail body. She resided in agony with every breath she took. In those moments, euthanasia did not seem like a bad idea. There was no cure and her conditions were terminal. Charlotte was hurting. Just when she and Betty Jo were getting comfortable as mother and daughter they would be separated again. Only this time she would not be taken from her mother, her mother would be taken from her, that was a tragedy. The brain tumors overwhelmed Betty Jo and she passed away, I was 12 years old when that happened.

Betty Jo's funeral consisted of friends and family that came from as far as Texas and Louisiana. Most of the faces were unfamiliar to me, I recognized Betty Jo's niece Carla and her two children Nikki and Carl. Carla was around Charlotte's age or a little older, Nikki and Shawnika were the same age, and Carl was about four years older than me. Ree did not show up, I searched the whole parlor for my Grandma's good friend. She was a heavyset, squat, brown skinned woman; she was always nice to me. When I was 4 years old, she gave me a little red chair that was just for me. I lugged that little red plastic chair around with me everywhere I went, so I could sit down anywhere, it was my personal throne. I loved that chair.

Charlotte got into an altercation with one of her estranged Aunts, Mabel. The fallout was over who would ride in the big limousine to the cemetery where Betty Jo would be buried. Charlotte assumed that herself, her husband, and kids would ride in the limo because after all she was Betty Jo's only child. Charlotte was sadly mistaken about that though, because Mabel did not care anything about that. Mabel said, "I grew up with Betty Jo, I knew her better than anybody, and she loved me more than anybody else alive." Bo convinced Charlotte to let Mabel have her way. The conflict was not worth it; the main objective was laying Betty Jo's body to rest. Mabel and Peter road in the big limo, while Charlotte road with us feeling totally rejected by the remaining members of her estranged family.

Nobody spoke up on her behalf. She was left nothing in the will, and Peter disappeared with everything to start his life over. Charlotte was not his biological daughter, and with Betty Jo gone he had no need or desire to continue dealing with her. She spiraled into a deep depression after that.

I do not know how, but shortly after that Charlotte found out that a woman in Philadelphia had just given birth to a baby boy that belonged to Bo. Charlotte drove Lincoln, Shawnika, and I over to Shawnika's Aunt CeCe who was an aunt to us too. Then she drove back to our small apartment on 3rd Ave and stabbed Bo repeatedly as she confronted him about the situation. Afterwards she went and drained out their bank account and took us to breakfast the next morning, as if nothing had happened. Luckily for the both of them he did not die, however he did have to spend quite some time in critical condition recovering. He refused to have charges pressed against Charlotte even though his mother insisted that he should. Despite what had occurred they stayed together and continued with their fractured marriage.

Charlotte kept on driving school buses and going to hair school in the evening. Bo healed up and went back to painting houses and buildings. Life was normal again, I guess. Shawnika, Lincoln, and I spent more time with Black's family; they helped with raising us. There were six members of their family: Grandma Mary, Aunt Cece, Black, and uncle's Jake, Byron, and Ron. Charlotte would prepare dinner and snacks for us. We would take them with us after school to Grandma Mary's house, so she wouldn't have to cook for us. She was already a senior citizen.

Despite all types of attempts to fix it, our life seemed to be bleeding out. At some point Bo and Charlotte, felt I was becoming uncontrollable. Bo accused me of stealing rent money which was later recovered. Before it was recovered, he got violent with me and bust my eardrum wide open. I balled my small fist and with eyes filled with tears wound up and caught him square on the jaw. Not only did it rock him, it shocked him. I had never fought him back before. I had enough, we stood there with our eyes locked in a loveless, angry stare. As if on cue, the super stepped out of his basement apartment with the payment receipt that he had forgotten to give me; in exchange for the money I brought to him.

How had this mix-up begun, you wonder? Bo asked me to bring the rent money down to Charles, the super of our building. He'd never asked me to do that before, nor gave me the instruction to get the receipt in exchange for the money. A day went by before he confronted me about the money. He brought me down to the

Super's place, knocked on the door which opened. He asked Charles where the money was. Charles replied saying, "what money?" Bo turned to me and just started hooking off with hard slaps and punches to my head and body. The super went back in, looked through his receipt box, found our receipt, brought it out; but it was too late, the damage had been done.

Charlotte took me to the Neighborhood Health Center to get my ear patched up. Bo and Charlotte discussed sending me to a state-run boy's home. Instead I ended up living with my estranged biological father who had been absent thus far, I was 14. The hardest part was leaving my brother and sister in that small apartment number 3C.

Charlotte resented my move which ended up in child custody court. The judge simply asked me "who do you want to be with?" I said my father and the case was closed. The last thing

Charlotte said to me that afternoon was "you are trading me in for someone who you do not even know." She was right.

Father

He was 26 years old when I came into the world. He and Charlotte were never a couple. They were only together long enough to conceive me. Months went by before he even knew I existed. Sharky already had a wife whom he had a daughter with. His wife was expecting another child by him who beat me to the world by 2 and a half weeks. Altogether Sharky had sired 8 children of which three are still missing in action. They do not know where he is at and he can't find them either. Two of the missing children he had helped to create, he did so while he was in the army. He was stationed at Fort Hood military base in Texas.

Besides having babies out there, two other life changing events happened to him. First, he was walking on his way to a girl's house, when he decided to take a shortcut through a field. He walked right into a Ku Klux Klan meeting. They tore his uniform off, broke several bones in his body, knocked him out, pissed on him, and left him for dead. The second incident struck less than a year after that beating. He was dishonorably discharged from the Army for trafficking heroin while in the service. They did not lock him up they just sent him on a long bus ride back to New York.

He was born in Harlem Hospital in 1952. He was one of 8 children the second oldest of four girls and four boys. His mother Louisa was Native American and his father Bobby African American. His father had retired from the Marine Corps and bought several pieces of property in Harlem where they lived. Three out of four of Bobby's sons went into the military. He smiled with great pride about building a legacy of military men. It broke his heart when he found out that Sharky had been kicked out of the military, which was in 1973. For a while he wanted nothing to do with Sharky. Back in New York with nothing to do, Sharky turned to drug dealing, drug abuse, gambling, pimping, cheating, stealing, conning people, and overall street life.

Bobby and Louisa wanted to get their kids out of Harlem, so they relocated to Mount Vernon which was 10 minutes away off the major Deegan Expressway North in Westchester County. They bought a three-family house to fit everybody into. They also bought a 10-unit apartment building that had multiple storefronts; properties that they could open for business or rent out. It was important for Louisa and Bobby to keep their family together. Although they were blessed to be able to change environments, Sharky refused to change his habits. He kept on drinking, drugging, and hustling. His drug of choice was heroin, he picked up the habit while in the Army. He entered the habit by sniffing it and graduated to shooting it in his veins.

Sharky's family home sat right around the corner from the foster home Charlotte stayed in. He would cruise down her street and honk the horn at her from behind the wheel of his Majestic Black 1976 Lincoln Continental Mark 4, with Truespoke Rims and Bogue Tires with the white and yellow trim. He always wore beautiful suits and jewelry. Sharky had been consumed with many bad habits however he remained a hustler who enjoyed luxury. Sharky hooked Charlotte and had his way with her right in her foster parents' home while no one was there. He found out from Charlotte's foster sister Pam that she had been shipped off to go live in a group home. Pam had also been the one to tell him that Charlotte had given birth to me. They went searching for Charlotte with his younger brother Derek and found her living in White Plains. Charlotte had found out about his wife and kids and decided she wanted nothing to do with him. In return he did not have much to do with me.

Sharky helped run a bar until it was shut down. Over a dozen dead bodies were discovered buried behind it. He was never tried or convicted for any of them. After that he landed a job with the public-school system doing custodial maintenance. He slowed down with the hustling, but his alcoholism and drug addiction continued being an important part of his life. He was a functioning addict. He and his wife divorced. His luxurious lifestyle declined as the years passed. He moved into the basement apartment of his family's apartment building. Nevertheless, he reached out to me and took a swing at being a father to his son. I accepted him as he was, he was my missing link.

DeShawn Kenner

Me: Under Mother's Roof

Summer times in California were great. Tommy, Shawnika's Grandad would take us to Magic Mountain, Great American, and SeaWorld just to name a few places. The first time traveling to Cali was a traumatic experience for my sister and I. Black and Charlotte drove us to LaGuardia Airport and put us on a plane bound for California's San Francisco Airport. They did not come with us and we had never seen or met Tommy. We were stressed, we could not stop crying. The flight attendants kept bringing us peanuts, sodas, and pillows; they tried to comfort us. This would be our first time away from Charlotte. Shawnika and I just held hands, and we cried ourselves to sleep. We felt like we were all that we had and could not let each other's hand go.

Tommy was at the gate as we exited the plane

escorted by the stewardesses. He said our names "Shamel, Shawnika." We walked over to him still holding hands. He bent down and hugged us both together. We also met Tommy's girlfriend Pearl, a brown-skinned voluptuous woman with a jheri curl. Tommy was a dark reddish Black with short cropped kinky hair, with a medium strong build, and he wore a pair of Terminator black shades. We retrieved our luggage from the spinning conveyor belt and left the airport.

He was driving the prettiest old car I had ever seen. He drove a light blue 1964 Impala with chrome rims, long white leather seats in the front and back seat of the car. We took the Golden Gate Bridge back to Oakland. The sun was setting when we pulled up on West 61st Street. Palm trees and houses lined the long block. He pulled into his driveway and parked behind his pickup truck.

Tommy's son and niece were in the house

when we walked in. It was a 1 level 2-bedroom house with a living room, dining room, bathroom, kitchen, front yard, backyard, and driveway with a garage which was filled with everything except for a car. The backyard had a lemon tree, fig tree, and marijuana plants growing next to the shed. He had a big black rusty-looking Rottweiler named Pale that did not mean any harm.

Tommy's son Tay and niece Christina instantly became the big brother and sister that Shawnika and I never had. He was 12 and she was 14. They were his West Coast family that had never been to New York. They took us everywhere with them. Tay's mother lived out in Berkeley, we would go to the beach up there often, we stayed on a corn dog diet.

Shawnika and I met Pearl's son Joe three Summers after the first one out there. Joe was from Chicago, he lived with his maternal grandmother, and he was as mean as a hungry lion. He and Tay were the same age. We boys would all watch WWF wrestling together. After the show we would do all the moves on each other. Being as I was the youngest, I got the short end of the stick. Joe was ruthless and suffocated me to the brink of death. If Shawnika tried to stop him, he would do it to her too. Tay also had a hard time. Christina would leave when he came around. He even slept with Tay's girlfriend. One morning I woke up and ran to the kitchen, I grabbed a small sharpened knife from the drawer. I planned on stabbing him up that day, but he never showed up. Turns out he went back to Chicago the night before.

Tommy owned some houses out there that were the original crack houses. Fiends and garbage everywhere, it was a small apartment complex. We would clean up the garbage around the property, pick up some more garbage from other sites around town, and take it all to the city dump. We would shovel, toss, and sweep the trash out of the back of the pickup truck. It smelled like everything rotten in the world was in there.

Coming back from California was always a transition for us; tranquility was more abundant out there for us than in New York, even with Joe's violence. The only thing missing while we were out there was Charlotte. As we drove up the major Deegan Expressway coming from JFK Airport watching the New York City skyline would reenergize me. New York's massive buildings and many lights on either side of the expressway commanded undivided attention. Having the George Washington Bridge in my eye sight reminded me of how far away we were from the Golden Gate Bridge. It was 7 hours and 10 minutes away on an American Airline flight, with one layover in Pittsburgh.

It seemed like our hood never changed. Loud music, loud people, drug dealers, altercations, and shootouts most of the day. When I heard gunshots, I would run to the window. Why? I felt like I was safe. No one was shooting at me. Violence was never random. There was always a reason and generally people did not go to the cops with their issues. As a matter of fact, I do not remember anyone calling the police for anything on my block. When they did come through, they were the enemy. I would soon find out why. All I knew was that you did not see, hear, or know anything even if you did. Meeting guys like Joe out in Cali let me know that there were violent people everywhere, not just at home.

Sadly, enough, we stopped going out to Cali because of a bad experience. Tommy and Pearl had separated. We had grown so much love for Pearl that we went out there to spend summers with her. She had a new man named Scotty. She was a nurse and a few nights a week she would work overnight at the hospital. She would leave us with Scotty. One night he climbed in the bed with my little sister and rubbed his hands on her body. Shawnika jumped out of the bed screaming and ran downstairs to where I was sleeping on the couch. She woke me up and let me know what happened. Scotty never came downstairs.

Shawnika and I sat on the couch. We were furious, it was like a violent thunderstorm existed inside of me. I was too young and too small to do something effective. We did not know Tommy's number, Pearl's number, Tay's number; nobody's number, but Charlotte's which was long distance and the phone was upstairs. We were trapped in the townhouse with a predator all night long. We were standing outside when Pearl pulled up into the parking lot. She parked and met us at the doorstep, we told her what happened. She went in the house to confront him. A dense heat soaked the morning air and the sun glowed brilliantly. We were a few doors down from Pearl's place standing with some other kids that were out bright and early in the morning. Suddenly, we saw Pearl come out of the house sprinting to her car and speed off right by us. We looked up and spotted Scotty standing there with a chrome handgun. Minutes later he came out of the place got in his car and left. I went back up to the house and called Charlotte, she called Tommy, and he showed up within the hour. He arrived in a van alone, Shawnika and I were beyond happy to see him. He went in with us to gather our belongings and then we exited the place.

One thing was for sure I was tired of feeling helpless or oppressed and at the mercy of older people. Tommy brought us back to Mount Vernon personally. That incident ended our vacations out in Oakland. We never laid eyes on

Pearl again or heard from her. She bounced on us without a second thought. I wondered if that was why Joe lived with his grandma or why he was so ill-tempered. Had she abandoned him too and was he jealous of her spending time with us? She neglected her own child, so how was she viewed as fit to be responsible for us? Just because you have money does not mean you are responsible. Ironically enough years later I found out Joe was sentenced to life for several homicides on the southside of Chicago.

In those years through the ages 9 to 12, I started to become conscious of how poor and vulnerable we were, and just how weak our family structure had been. Charlotte received public assistance which meant we were too. Our two bedrooms on the third floor was not the palace that I once saw it as. Shawnika, Lincoln, and I were getting big and the room we shared smaller. The things I took in through my eyes now looked different in my mind. The raw reality of my life started to reveal itself. Sadness overwhelmed me at times to the point where I was depressed and could not stop crying because of the pain I felt inside. I did not want to be here anymore.

I would not ask Charlotte for much because I knew she did not really have it to give me. I remember times she would give me a dollar and I would feel like a millionaire. Now if she gave me a buck, I knew it was half of what she had. I did not even want it, taking it seemed selfish of me. I stopped bothering with school field trips, because they cost money. I refrained from asking Big Bo for anything as well. I knew he was not my real father. I felt in my heart that if anything happened to Charlotte like death, he would leave us for dead. Charlotte kept him there, not us. I secretly thought that he hated us. When he beat me, it came from the place of hate and resentment because we were not his, as if we were in the way of his and my mom's perfect life.

I could not help but feel like unwanted luggage to him. My choice to go live with Sharky had two main goals. One was to get to know my father and two was to ease some economic burden on Charlotte. The time had arrived for me to leave her nest. I love Charlotte and always will.

DeShawn Kenner

Me and Education

I loved school, got great grades, and stayed on the honor roll. I played instruments, the flutophone which is a small beginner's flute, the saxophone, the snare drums, and the bass drum. Education and learning gave me peace and confidence. Even something as simple as being able to spell and write my own name made me happy. I remember when I would scribble on paper as if I were writing out my whole government. It would frustrate me not knowing how to do it. It also insulated me with confidence to do something as challenging as write this book that you are reading.

With grief and sorrow I sadly tell you that I failed to graduate high school or go on to an ivy league university as I had planned to all so long ago. Here's the short version of what happened. I was expelled for not complying with a teacher's request. What was his request? He just asked me to go to class, that was all.

I was lingering in the hallway with a guy I barely knew in between class periods. We were trying to out cool each other, meaning we were discussing who was cooler out of the two of us, and who had more swag. The educator walked up on both of us and said "don't you have somewhere to be? Go to class." The idiot that was standing there said to the teacher, "f*** you!" We stood there confrontationally as if it was nothing. Peer pressure controlled me at that point. Deep in my heart I knew I should've kept it moving, but I didn't.

We were all standing there awkwardly. The teacher had a stack of xerox copies in one arm and a cup of coffee in his other hand. He dropped everything and rushed us. We took off, he pursued us, and shouted, "you cannot outrun me, I run marathons!" At some point, us two troublemakers split up. Guess who he kept chasing, me! A security guard joined his hunt. They caught up with me, we had a tussle, it got violent, and that was the end of my high school career. They wanted to have me arrested, however I left before the official police showed up. Mount Vernon High School was experiencing stabbings, shootings, assaults, and other crimes in its hallways and staircases. Due to those happenings they had been demonstrating a zero-tolerance clause for school misbehavior.

Just like that, everything I had worked for and toward in school went down the drain. I had previously spoken in front of the city council for neighborhood environmental issues, in Junior High School, because my English teacher Ms. Perkins knew I was well-spoken. She even came to my dangerous block to pick me up for the event. I had also traveled to the nation's capital to sing on the steps of Capitol Hill with my class. All of this seemed lost now and no 'A' that I had ever earned would count for anything. Life had changed as I knew it and there would be no returning to old times.

Ironically, Sharky had never known that my school days were over. I mention this because he had custody of me, my father was my guardian, I lived with him. I was fifteen when that occurred, I had just entered the 10th grade, my sophomore year. I will get back to life after that terrible decision, but before I do, I am going to explain life under Sharky's roof.

Under Sharky's Roof

I had met one of Sharky's sisters Sylvia and her son Barry when I was in kindergarten. Charlotte would take me by their house, and we would just sit around trying to figure each other out until it was time to leave. Charlotte escorted me to Sharky's mother's funeral somewhere around that time as well. Everyone in attendance had been an unfamiliar face to me, even Sharky's mom. I was ushered up to the casket to view her. She was a pretty light skinned lady with long silver hair. She seemed to be resting peacefully with a smile on her face. Everyone around me was in tears mourning her. That had been the first time that I had been amongst that many of those family members.

The next time that I saw that family and a heavy crowd was when his father put together a family cookout at his home. He invited me, Charlotte dropped me off at his house. I was nervous and uncomfortable; I had met him before briefly. Charlotte had brought me by the beauty parlor/barber shop that he owned and operated. He and Sharky seemed like night and day. My grandfather was a handsome, well-kept man, with a very strong presence, and build even for an older man. He always made me feel like I belonged to his family. We had a natural connection, so Charlotte would try to leave me with him, however I refused. I was not ready at that time, I still happened to be a deeply committed mama's boy. During the years leaving her to go to Cali was difficult enough. Bobby said, "when you are ready, I'll be here."

Sharky had a presence, however it did not compare to the presence of his dad for me. At the cookout I made my rounds. He introduced me to his three daughters; Stacy, Nene, and Lena;

and his other son Sharky Jr. Oddly enough I had seen Nene in school, we were the same age. I remembered Sharky Jr. as well. Sharky had come to pick me up from Grandma Mary's house when I was younger, he had Sharky Jr. with him. He took us both to the bar that he ran. The place smelled funny, it smelled like cigar smoke and alcoholism. Sharky Jr. and I sat on high stools playing Pacman all night. I do not remember how or when I left there. I had fallen asleep with my head resting on the arcade game.

I met my cousin Tricia and I had a fight with my cousin Barry. He tried to style on me because he had the home-court advantage. He had grown up with and around these people, I did not. That did not stop me from kicking his butt. At thirteen years old I had my weight up. I used Big Bo's dumbbells regularly and little had Barry known that I fought all the time. The south side of Mount Vernon was rough. My block 3rd Avenue was the roughest. You had to know how to fight or you would get beat up all the time. Barry and I got tight after that though. He would even come to visit me at Charlotte's house, he could even spend the night if he wanted to if his mother knew. Barry was in the street though, he peddled crack in the projects. He and I were the same height; however, I had more size than him. He was 3 years older than me.

At the end of the cookout Bobby grabbed my hand with a firm gentle grip looked me in the eye and said, "come back to see me." I said, "all right," and I meant it. Two weeks later he passed away, he had a military send-off, we all went. I found out that he was a Mason. His Mason brothers showed up, sang for him, and paid homage. He was buried in Calverton, Long Island which has a military cemetery. They played Taps, folded the flag that had been draped over his casket, and gave it to Sharky's sister Minnie;

because she would be the heir to his assets.

I grew to love Minnie, however she and my father never got along. She did not hold her beef with him against me though. Minnie taught me about business. She had earned a business degree from Cornell University and worked on the side as an accountant. She lived in the same apartment building as Sharky; while he lived in the beat-up basement, she lived on the top floor with her son Nick who at the time was a toddler. Nene and I stayed in the basement, however everybody frequented the place. All our friends, cousins, sisters, and brothers chilled out down there. Sharky was hardly ever there. He stayed at different girlfriend's houses, and I saw why.

The basement reminded me of a cross between a hideout and a crack house. The windows had plastic on them in place of glass. The carpet looked worn out and filthy. There was no sheetrock or cover for the ceiling, in the living room or the two bedrooms. The appearance of the doors were tired. The refrigerator had nothing in it, but old moldy plates wrapped in aluminum foil. Those were leftovers Sharky would bring for us to eat or for him to snack on when he would stop by. The phone didn't work. There were holes in all the places that rodents could come and go as they pleased. The beds and couch were dirty, and linens needed to be washed. The walls had wood paneling, it was always cold down there, and the motor of something banged 24 hours a day. I could go on and on about that place.

Charlotte's place was immaculate compared to that place. Charlotte's place was nice but restricted; the basement was a disaster, but I was free. A lot came with my new independence. Sharky showed up on the weekends and made us egg omelets with cheese, peppers, onions, and sausage. Usually that was when we would connect, then he disappeared again with no way to be contacted other than the school he worked at. Nene went up the hill to her mother's house when it got too rough there. My pride would not allow me to go crawling back to Charlotte for help. I had made my decision and I had to deal with it. I had no money, new clothes, anything to eat, or direction. I needed to do something. Barry came by and brought me some food and gave me a couple dollars to spend wisely, I was thankful for him. I went to different friends' houses to eat, take a decent nap, and if I were lucky wash my clothes.

DeShawn Kenner

Community

Mount Vernon was a Melting Pot of African American, African Caribbean, Hispanic, Italian, and Jewish settlers mainly. Overall it had a predominantly Black population. Since I have been alive every mayor elected has been African-American or Jamaican. For the sake of space on the paper until I restate the definition when I say Americans, I will be referring to Black Americans. Growing up we never discussed the use of the n word, it was just used. It is funny to me though I must admit that when you ask Black people from anywhere outside of the USA where they are from or what their nationality is, they will just say Puerto Rican, Haitian, Jamaican, Dominican, Cuban, etc. On the contrary, Blacks born in America usually give a two-part answer such as African American or Black American.

Going a step further we may just drop our nationality and just say "I am Black". Paraphrasing W.E.B. Dubois, we in America live a duality of being African and American at the same time. If it is a nationality issue why if we are born here, must we stress two?

Many Americans and Jamaicans did not get along when I was growing up. There was a type of ethnic and cultural racism that existed. They would refer to each other's groups with disrespectful name-calling. Americans would call them coconuts and booty scratchers, while Jamaicans would use names such as yankees and blood clots. It seemed like most were concerned more with nationality than race. I got along well with everyone for the most part. Whenever I did have an issue with someone or a group; it has never been because of their race, ethnicity, or nationality most of my fights stem from disrespect. Disrespect has no specific color, race, height, language, religion, or address; it resides everywhere. Disrespect can be viewed as bullying another person, degrading another person, or taking advantage of another person in an egregious way without their consent. People who take kindness for weakness are the worst. Many nice people have stopped being the nice people they really were, because someone had taken their generosity for granted one too many times. That's sad because the world needs nicer, calming, loving, helpful people in it. As a kid, what went on in my household had me contemplating my nice guy mindset at heart. I am a good guy, however two incidents happened in my community that helped me take off my exterior layer of niceness.

The first incident happened when I was 13 years old. Charlotte worked for the bus company during the day. From 4 p.m. until 8 p.m. Monday through Friday she would be at hair school.

Generally, in my neighborhood no one called the police for anything. Their presence had been more harmful than helpful. I was about to find out why that ideal existed. One day Charlotte had left us a couple of dollars to get some snacks from the corner store before she left for school. I finished my homework and left out to go get our snacks. It was winter, snow had been falling madly to the ground. Outside felt like the inside of an icebox. Ms. Perry's Corner Store was five buildings away from mine in a corner store front. I disregarded my coat, long sleeve shirt, or socks for my quick dip to the store. I figured I would be there and back before Jack Frost could touch me. Instead, one building away from the store a Yellow Cab pulled up beside me, two hulking men jumped out of the car. One Black guy and one white guy approached me quickly with guns drawn, they commanded me to stop walking while pressing the barrels of their guns against either side of my ribs. They hurriedly ushered me into the back seat of their car, I had just been abducted.

I sat in between these two strangers in the back seat while the driver sped off with my life. It all happened in the blink of an eye. I was not only shocked, but also gripped by a confused silence. The guy in the front picked up and talked into the transmitter of the car radio. I couldn't fully make out the message he relayed, but I clearly remember him calling me a perp. I spotted a badge, one of my abductors had pulled it out from underneath his shirt. They were cops. I thought to myself, what are police doing in street clothes and why aren't they in uniform? We arrived at the station. They pulled me out of the back of the taxi, cuffed my hands behind my back, and led me through a side door. We went into a big office with four or five desks, where there was also a small holding cell. One of them released me from the cuffs and pushed me into the small cage.

They instructed me to take my clothes off, I refused. They said I would not be leaving there until I stripped naked. I told them I needed to call my mother. The officer said, "f**** your mother! She cannot help you, nothing will happen until you take those clothes off." I occupied that cage for three hours until I reluctantly got naked, bent over, spread my butt cheeks, lifted my genitals, showed them the inside of my mouth, and let them search my clothes. They threw my clothes and sneakers back into the tiny cell and watched me get dressed. They smiled, laughed, and cracked jokes as if they had taken pride in humiliating me. I could not help thinking that they were gay, because they never took their eyes off me the whole time I was getting dressed. I had never felt that naked in my life.

Their personalities had changed. They started talking to me as if they had known me my whole life and loved me. Anger befriended me. They acted as if I had no reason to be angry. I had become the a****** with the unnecessary attitude. They never even told me why I had been abducted. All I knew for sure was that I had been labeled a perp. One of them shoved me out of the side door and said, "stay from up there." How could I have stayed from up there? I lived up there. It had grown colder outside. The night had become darker. It took me a half hour to make it home. During that march home, I had thought about telling Charlotte and Big Bo what happened to me. I wanted a lawyer, I had been violated for no reason at all.

When I made it upstairs, Shawnika and Lincoln were still the only ones there. Shawnika was in our room listening to music and Lincoln laid in Charlotte's bed watching TV. They had not even asked me about the snacks. Life had gone on. Charlotte came in 5 minutes behind me. The first things she said were, "why are there dishes in my sink, and take the garbage out now." She came in beefing and annoyed. Right then in that moment I decided to keep what happened to me to myself. The cop had been right. Charlotte young poor mother of three whose concerns had been dishes in her sink, garbage in her apartment, cooking dinner, her bus job, hair school, and a cheating husband; could not help me. It would've only been another piece of stress to help to break her down further than she already had been. That reality had been as cold as the weather that I had just been freezing in. I had heard others say it before, however that would be the first time I said it and sincerely meant it, f*** the police!

After that incident I never felt like cops were there to serve and protect me.

The only other officer that I had contact with

before that was officer Gooden. He had come to my elementary school and taught the DARE program to my class every Friday afternoon. DARE stood for Drug Abuse Resistance Education. His lessons were about how kids could stay off illegal drugs. He had already made me leery of cops. He pushed kids around and placed them under arrest if they talked while he was giving his spiel. That created fear of police in me, in us all, not a relationship of respect or admiration for cops. No wonder many of those kids still grew up and tried drugs anyway, including me. I smoked marijuana, cigarettes, cigars, drank beer, and hard liquor. I even ended up a drug trafficker, we will get to that later.

The second situation that made me take off my mister nice guy shell was right after my 14th birthday. I had just stepped off the city bus coming from school when I encountered a life-threatening situation. I had entered my block and headed for Charlotte's apartment, but before I reached my building I had come face-to-face with a grim reaper. A guy I had never seen before was standing in front of a building I walked past. Instantly we made eye contact. Defensively I asked him "who are you and why are you over here?" Without warning or hesitation, he pulled out a small machine gun from underneath his black hooded sweatshirt and started to approach me, with it pointed directly at me. I was only a few steps away from him. He could have just opened fire on me, but he did not. His intention was to get right up on me. We never lost eye contact. I did not run. I stood there watching him approach me, my body went numb. At the last moment someone stepped in between us. It felt like divine intervention. It was Father Divine, he said to my would-be assassin that I was good. The gun man put the gun back under his shirt and went back onto the steps of the building he was standing in front of. We had not broken eye contact as Father Divine escorted me up the block to my building. He told me to go upstairs and to not come back out because it was about to get hot.

Divine was an OG to me. He was in his early twenties into heavy drug trafficking, murder, and robbery in and out of NYS. Everybody knew what he was about; he was loved, respected, feared, and hated. Before he was known as a shooter, he was known as a vicious fighter who had beat up everybody he ever fought. I had seen him fight a few times, he never lost in front of me. I felt great pride in knowing him and great pride that we were from the same block.

When I was growing up people around the way respected and feared a person male or female if they could fight really well. They would even show love to the person who fought back, even if they could not fight well. The ideology was at least they went out; however, no one respected a coward. You were a target if you were a coward, subject to limitless disrespect. I did not want to be the target of disrespect, so I fought whenever I had to. Yet there were those who were more feared and respected than fighters. They were people known to use weapons, namely knives and guns. If you were known for stabbing, cutting, or shooting; people were not quick to try you. There were those who could fight but did not use weapons nor did they want problems with someone who used weapons. They stayed in their fistfight lane.

There were levels to knife wielders too. If you were a person who just got off cutting people across the face, it was recognized that you were not trying to kill anyone. The face slasher did not want beef with someone who would stab him or shoot him; they stayed in their slasher lane. There were still differences, you had people who would only use knives and would've stabbed you to death but did not use guns.

The next few levels up became more dangerous. There were those who used guns, there were three types of gun carriers. The first type carried a gun to scare you and for show. If and when they shot, they only did so in the air or at imaginary targets. They never hit anybody except by accident. You had to watch them because they were reckless. The second type of gun man would shoot you, but their intentions were not to kill you. Generally, they would shoot at your lower body in places like the foot, leg, and butt of a person. The third type would shoot you in the head and chest, to kill you. They controlled all lanes and levels in the streets and were the most feared and respected; even amongst killers there were levels.

The highest levels were reserved for the most dangerous killers who were smart, respectful, alphas, who got money, and could do all the above. They were well disciplined, blended in, stayed well-kept, went anywhere, and connected with different crowds. They were the all-stars of the street. Divine was an All-Star. He had done it all and was charismatic while doing it. Just because you were a killer did not mean you were about your money or even smart. There were bummy killers who got drunk and high all day. They had done nothing else with their lives but wait for beef, theirs or someone else's.

There were various other types of killers running around. The two most common in the hood were the ones that would killed you for their money and disrespect of family, and the ones who would kill you for next to nothing, over something as simple as a female who may be cheating on him with you or stepping on their shoes. They felt they had a reputation to protect and did not want to be seen as a joke. I never forgot the look in my would-be killer's eyes or what it said to me. What the look in his eyes said to me was that my life meant nothing to him. He would take it from me, and I would never get it back. I can still see his cold stare in my mind.

I had been upstairs for about 20 minutes when like 100 gunshots rang out. Divine was American, he had a feud going with some Jamaican guys from around the corner. After the shots had stopped two men had died. I never saw my would-be murderer again. He was not among the fatalities, nor would be. They said the shooting happened over business gone wrong. Divine had a rapport with some of the Jamaican boys, so much so that he had taken a few of them to Atlanta with him to get money. They robbed and killed a dude that Divine had introduced them to, then they left without telling him anything. They just left him holding the short end of the stick. The Southern Boys loved D though.

He had been out there for years, they had become family. They had known he had nothing to do with what happened to their kinfolk. His only crime was bringing those grimy none trustworthy dudes out there with him. He had to make things right. He found them back in the hood and brought war to them.

That night up in Charlotte's tiny apartment I decided I would be a shooter. Charlotte could not protect me. The police could not be trusted to protect me, they had become the enemy too. I had to stand up for myself and my people. I never went looking to take somebody out after that personal revelation. I just knew it could've happened, I had not even had a gun.

My Transformation

When I relocated to Sharky's basement my life begun its transformation. Within a year of being there I had four guns, was no longer in school, I had committed a few robberies, and had moved on to selling crack and cocaine. I received my guns from three older dudes that I looked up to.

Speedy gave me a 32 caliber seven shot automatic. Speedy was a Jamaican old timer who sold weed in the hood. I had known him since I was in first grade, he had a daughter that was in my class. He had liked my mother. I always went to her birthday parties and she came to mine.

I walked into his store front weed spot and told him I had beef I needed to handle. He had always told me that if I had any problems to come see him. Without hesitation, he reached across the counter and handed me my first gun.

He gave me three instructions: first don't tell anyone that he gave it to me, second don't bring it back, and finally all I needed to do was point it at the person and pull the trigger.

The second gun I got was from Sha, he gave me a 9mm to hold down. He had done eight years in prison for a manslaughter charge he caught when he was 16. He was originally from Fort Green Brooklyn, his mother lived in Mt Vernon. While in prison he joined the Nation of Islam N.O.I. We boxed at the same gym. He was a big brother to me. Sha had struggled with doing the right thing. I was thirteen when we met, he had just come home. When I moved to Sharky's house, I let him know. Sharky's neighborhood was a bit more tamed than Charlotte's. Sha was on parole, we agreed that it was better to keep the nine in the basement. He really did not want it or to go back up north. I did not want him to go back up north. Myself on the other hand was not thinking anything about prison, even when he explained the horrors of it to me. My mind was made up and I would have to learn things my own way, even if that would be the hard way.

Sha sold clothes and coats. We took the train downtown into Manhattan. He purchased his merchandise on West 27th St. and then re-sold it in downtown Brooklyn on Fulton St. He tried to give me the hustle, I just could not get with it. He tried to take me to the Million-Man March and I ducked him. I was not with it. Sha got more into NOI and love for Black people. I got more into the street and disregarding Black life; even though my own life was Black.

The last two of the first four guns I received came from Powerful. He gave me a double barreled sawed off shot gun and a police issued 38 Revolver. Powerful taught me my first real lessons about the street game. He was a Five Percenter which represents the Nations of Gods and Earths. Their purpose is to live consciously and practice self-reliance; not by the perception that was placed upon their slave ancestors who were considered mentally dead. They also believe that the Black man is God and the White man is the Devil, simply stated. Powerful introduced me to drug dealing. He was my mother's age and Father Divine's older brother. He was one of my boxing trainers. His specialty fighting style was called the fifty-two. It was a boxing style started and developed in prison. Powerful had been one of the founding fathers of that style. He was a drug lord in the 80's. He had put Father Divine and various dudes onto hustling crack and heroin. He ended up getting shot several times at a Go-Go Club in Washington DC. He walked with a limp because of that incident. He had also been the person who told me Charlotte was using drugs, namely crack.

One night after we trained at the center,

Powerful asked me what was going on with me. I told him that I did not live with Charlotte anymore and that I now stayed with my father who I barely knew or saw. I let him know that I was hurting, bad was becoming worse. I do not know where I even found the energy to box from, because I was not eating right. He felt my pain. He also knew my cousin Barry who was in Federal Prison for drug dealing. He took me to his house, I sat in his nicely decorated living room. He came back from another room with a plastic shopping bag filled with something. He poured the contents out onto a round glass coffee table that sat in front of the couch we were sitting on. He counted five hundred glass vile yellow topped capsules, that were worth ten dollars each. He gave me 250 of them and told me that we were partners. He added on that I was to never work for anybody. I could work with people but never for them. He said, "forget the fame, just get the fortune. It was about hustling to have, not to be known. The less you were known, the longer you would last."

It all happened so fast, I did not even know where to sell it. He told me to go up on Charlotte's block. Then he decided to walk me through the process. He took me to my old block, we entered the building right across the street from Charlotte's. He rang a bell, someone buzzed us in. We went into Linda's apartment on the 1st floor. I had known her my whole life, and I knew she did drugs. He told her I had work. He told me to give her one to sample, I gave it to her, she smoked it right there. I had never seen crack smoked before, let alone right in front of me. It had a strong rank odor. It must have been good, because Linda pulled out a twenty-dollar bill and said, "give me two more." After that it was history. It seemed like all the older people I looked up to and had known as a kid were strung out on crack, cocaine, heroin, weed, cigarettes, and alcohol. That included Big Bo and Charlotte. I never sold to them, I just knew that they were addicted. The world seemed different to me now. As if I had been lied to my whole life or was just ignorant to see the truth of what had been really happening around me.

My whole life had been submerged in a drug infestation. Drugs ravaged not just my neighborhood but my household, I had not even known it. That is why I had not seen much of Sharky, he had been chasing his habit. I had been accepted as a young drug dealer in my hood, because I was from there and had grew up fighting for the blocks honor and my own. Remember cowards got no respect. I had developed a fearless reputation for myself thus far. It was enough to get me in the game. The streets embraced me and were happy to have me.

Being a stick-up kid was not for me. It was

high risk with uncertain reward most of the time. The last robbery I committed with two accomplices did not turn out well, two people were shot. One of the guys I partnered up with got blasted and one of the guys we sought to take from got hit. We ran up in a bodega/gambling spot. We entered the store, one of my crime partners a tall lanky guy threw the barrel of the nine into the face of the clerk at the counter. Me and my other team mate ran to the back of the store, my buddy opened the door and we rushed in. My heart was racing. I had anxiety, adrenaline, and the jitters going on inside of me at the same time, but there was no turning back. Some of our victims were not cooperating. Liquor bottles lined the tables they were at, reefer smoke lingered in the air, most of them were drunk, and high. We pistol whipped a few of them and scrapped up sixty-two hundred dollars before we exited. We were not out of the store five seconds before one of them opened fire on us. They struck the guy I went in the back with twice. One shot landed high on the back side of his left shoulder, the other shot struck him dead in the center of his back, he fell instantly.

Slim and I made it to an alley way outside the line of fire. However, our friend Fingers laid lifelessly on the icy cold street. I knew Fingers my whole life, our mothers were friends. We spent nights at each other's houses. We fought against each other and others. I could not just leave him there. More gun fire erupted, they shot at him while he was on the ground. Impulsively I ran out of the alley and shot off both barrels of the 12 gauge, forcing the other two-gun men to scramble for cover. Even though they had guns they still respected gun fire coming their way. I went back into the alley. Slim started to panic. I could not get the shot gun to open so I could reload it. I handed it to Slim, so he could try to force it open. The temperature had dropped. I could not feel my fingers. I looked out of the alley over to where Fingers had been laying, he started Screaming my government name, "Shamel, Shamel!!" I saw a gunman creeping up on Fingers. I ordered the nine from Slim, he passed it to me. I lost all sense of danger and ran toward the guy shooting. He shot right back at me. He fell a few feet from Fingers. I do not know where I got the strength from, but I tossed Fingers over my shoulders and jogged off with him over slippery ice. I made it to the alley with him. Slim had disappeared. I had made it down the alley across the street into another one, when reality set in. If any of those guys with a gun had become brave enough to venture into that alley, we could've died. It was a very vulnerable moment. Fingers had been bleeding all over the place, he had his finger nails dug deep in my neck. I had a gun in my hand trying to balance myself and him coming across snow and ice. I had become beyond exhausted, fatigue had set in. I carried him six long blocks, a cop car had just missed us at one point. We made it to the stash spot. Slim was there, three of our other affiliates were there, all hell had broken loose. The money did not even seem important at that point.

I got Fingers off the scene of the crime, but now it was time for me to get up out of there. Two things happened after I left: 1) the police tracked the trail of blood and 2) Fingers had already left in route to Jacobi Hospital in the Bronx. He was arrested fresh out of surgery. He had been sentenced to fifteen years for that jooks. He was 15 years old with 15 years to do. I must say, he never snitched us out.

After that whole ordeal, robbery lost its luster to me. I already didn't like the idea of it, but now I really did not like it. Robbery had been Slim and Fingers' thing. My heart was never fully committed to it. It was not how or why I wanted to take a life. I had invited them to sell crack with me, however they declined. They reasoned they did not have time for all that slow drug selling and counting business, it was too much. They wanted to let someone else make the money and take it from them, simple. I learned the hard way, what I believe I already knew, nothing was that simple. People who were getting money, that you intended to rob were not going to make it easy for you, nine times out of ten. You may go on a jooks with hopes of catching hundreds of thousands and get nothing. You may also get a bullet and/or jail time instead. It was a risky toss-up.

I fell in love with drug dealing, for me it had its risks but not the same as robbery. Drug dealing ran like any other business, a product for sale. It is a mutual agreement between dealer and purchaser. You had a product and they wanted to buy it, no one needed to get hurt for the transaction. I would rather kill someone protecting while building and earning my own interest, than by taking them out to take theirs.

I secretly was sad and disappointed with myself about my first shooting. I could spin the story in my mind and say Fingers remained alive because of my actions, but another man had been laid down. Ultimately because we went to take what belonged to him. Nothing about it felt right to me. That situation taught me something about myself, I was not ready to be the killing machine that I thought I would be. I had a heart that grieved for a person that I did not know. The deeper revelation that I discovered was that I just wanted to eat. Meaning that I could have and afford decent food, clothing, and shelter, that was it.

The drug game allowed me to do things and have things at my young age that otherwise I would not have been able to afford. Things as simple as going out to eat when I wanted, I could have a burger and fries, or a slice of pizza whenever I wanted. I could afford to look out for my brother and sisters, especially Shawnika and Lincoln. I would take them school shopping, food shopping, or just be able to put some dollars in their pockets, that felt great to me. I sold cocaine, crack, heroin, and marijuana. Powerful had passed away, he overdosed on heroin. I would take the number 2 train to 96th Street to come back uptown to 135th St on the number 1 train. I would then walk to 139th street and Broadway to re-up with fresh cocaine, (fish scale).

The block sat on a hill in between Broadway and Riverside Drive. I went to go see Felix. He became my drug dealing mentor. I met Felix on 140th between Amsterdam and Hamilton Place while I was with Powerful. He made sure I knew all the spots to go re-up at. Re-upping meant to go buy more drugs to sell at good low prices, so I could turn out profits. He made sure they all knew me or at least recognized my face. Powerful brought me to Johnny a supplier he had known over twenty years, Felix was with him. Felix was just a little older than me, eighteen or nineteen at the time. I could tell Johnny was grooming him, just like Powerful was grooming me. Johnny and Powerful joked about Felix and I looking like brothers or cousins, we laughed too. We were the same complexion, a light brown skin. By nationality he sided Dominican and I with American. He spoke English perfectly though, like he was from the hood too. He was well mannered like me. We always showed each other respect and love.

Something happened to Johnny where he got locked up, then deported back to the Dominican Republic. Felix took over and moved the operation down the hill from Amsterdam to Broadway. He showed me a lot of love. He had some guys in a building with calculator watches adding up and multiplying the number of grams people like me wanted to buy. He only sold weight. The weight depended on how much it cost for a gram of fish scale. At that time grams were going for $18, so that meant one ounce would cost $504, which was the equivalent to 28 grams. You could buy a whole Kilo for $18,000, which was 1000 grams or $18/gram. He probably got his product at $13/gram. While his guys were in the building doing business, he sat in his minivan or car across the street watching the traffic go in and out the spot. Some days I sat in the car with him, sometimes all day, other times a couple of hours. We would just be talking about the drug game, girls, family, and goals. He would tell his boys I was his little brother. He liked me, he said I was young, selling for myself, and I was always by myself. I learned that from Powerful. He told me never to be in a crowd because all it did was draw attention.

One day Felix and I had a conversation. I asked him was he going back to DR and was it better than America. He said, "when you have money you can go wherever you want to go. Anywhere you go it is the same. If you have money you are good, and if you do not have money you are hungry. They do not make Uzis or grow cocaine in DR either." That was funny to me because there is a scene in New Jack City where Nino Brown said something similar about drugs and guns in Harlem, that they did not make Uzis in Harlem. Felix said he goes where the money goes, if it went to another planet, then he was out of here; we laughed.

Felix was murdered shortly after that. He was shot twice in his head, I still do not know why. All I do know is that when I went through 139th and Broadway; the block was blocked off by police barricades, and no people or cars could enter that street. It was even crazier to me when I saw his picture on channel 7 eyewitness news. Even though he had died he and two hundred other Dominicans from that area had been indicted for drug related homicides. I stopped going up around there altogether. I learned that the guard in the streets changed quickly. As soon as they were gone, and the coast was clear another 'Felix' popped up and another team replaced his.

The game did not nor does stop for anybody. That included me because I kept it moving forward with the business of drug dealing. Next level extraordinary and successful drug dealers had spots out of town, outside of Mt Vernon. Too many hustlers congested the corners, too many addicts had short money, and there was not a good economy there to supply good paying jobs. The two main legal job providers were the school district (teacher, crossing guard, security, bus drivers, and janitors.) The other was the medical field (nurses, nurse's aide, orderlies, home health aides, etc.) Besides privately-owned family businesses like pizza shops, Chinese restaurants, sneaker stores, hat shops, beef patty shops, barber shops, music stores, and grocery stores, to name a few, Welfare and the drug game were the main money pipelines. There had always been heavy competition for scarce resources. Demand for jobs had always been greater than the supply and availability of them.

Intelligent hustlers understood that dynamic. They took their product where competition was little or none and demand for it was beaming at all-time highs. It was like being a bear with a private salmon stream. However, transporting and selling work in another environment outside of your town came with more risk. When you entered another town, city, borough, state, or country you lost your home court advantage. You didn't know the people, places, or how they did things. If someone brought you out there you did not know what they had been into out there, or how the public perceived them.

Out-of-Town

The first time I tried my hand out of town, I went to Boston with a kid named Pillz. His grandmother lived there. He said the money out there was serious. He had me by 2 years, I was fifteen. I stuffed five hundred grams of wrapped up fish scale into a Jansport book bag, and added a 357 Smith-n-Wesson to it that I had wrapped up in a thick sweater. I brought a thousand dollars spending cash for room, board, transportation, and food. It was to last until we made some sales.

I paid our way out there, we took the Amtrak from New Rochelle. Pillz did not have any money, he just had ambition and the spot. He was the scout; his responsibility was to have somewhere for us to set up shop and run some customers. If all went well, I would give him a big eigth which is one hundred twenty-five grams, that would help him get on his feet. We would make some moves together, but he would have to earn it; that never happened.

When we arrived in Boston it was a little after six in the evening. We took a cab to some Spanish girl's house, which was an apartment in a rundown house. She did not even know we were coming. In her eyes we just popped up on her. She looked extra short standing next to Pillz tall dark muscular frame. She was very cute. She let us in, she was in the house with an infant and a toddler. Her name was Lisa. Pillz was the father of her baby boy, but not her three-year-old daughter. He went to the back with her for a few minutes. I went to look out her window from behind the closed window pane. It was a nice view of the street which consisted of the pedestrians and cars passing by. She lived on a long narrow one-way street. He emerged from the back alone and asked me for fifty dollars. I did not ask why, I just gave it to him, I figured it had something to do with our sleeping arrangements. We would camp out there for the night, that had been the plan.

Around two in the morning somebody started ringing her bell. She slipped out of the back bedroom where she and Pillz were laid up, walked over to the window, and looked out. She hustled back to her room, came back out in a red sweat suit and boots, and hurried out the door. Instinctively I peeked out of the window. She had three burly dudes in her face. I hustled my trey pound out of the book bag. I did not know if we were being set up, if there was a problem brewing, or what. All I knew was that the time had come to be up and ready. Pillz stepped out of the shadows of the back room and asked me where she went, I told him outside. He went to the window took a glance, then rushed outside to her. I was fully dressed and ready to roll. I posted up by the window and stared out of it waiting to see what would happen. His presence surprised them all. He had his chest out being really animated as if he were about to do something. I watched it play out in slow motion and could not stop it.

While he was arguing with one of the guys another one of them shot Pillz repeatedly with a gun that had been concealed in his coat pocket. He never actually pulled the thing out. Pillz took off running past them and collapsed on the other side of the street. Lisa ran over to where he had just laid out. The three guys started casually walking down the street as if nothing had just happened. I backed away from the window in disbelief. Being honest I have to say that fear gripped me at the very core of my existence in that moment.

In the next moment, I had begun creeping out the door to the sidewalk. I did not go check on Pillz. Instead I made the sharp right that his assailants had taken with my gun out cocked. They were gangsta strolling slowly like they did not have a care in the world. I had a nice paced power walk going for myself, I caught up with them in no time. They never looked back, so they did not see me coming. I raised my gun up to the back of the trigger man's head. I knew it was him, because he had been the only one wearing a black knitted hat. I shot twice right through it. I then turned the pound on the other two striking them high up in the chest and face while I still had the drop or the element of surprise.

They both ran off, one in between two parked cars. The other one just kept going, who knows maybe I didn't hit him. I did not stick around to find out either. I had spent all five shots. I sprinted back to where Pillz had been, and I kept looking back the whole time. Paranoia shook me up. He was not in the street anymore.

Lisa pulled up on me in a light blue Honda Accord. At first, I ducked then realized it was her and Pillz. I climbed in the backseat. She put it in reverse and backed out of the block. He died in the car. I kissed him on the back of the head and said a silent prayer for him.

I did not know what possessed me to say a prayer, but I did. She was driving and crying. I was in the back seat feeling sick to my stomach. She and I did not know each other; however, we had forged an instant bond made of pain and loss. She pulled over in front of a house about ten minutes away from where we had just escaped. She told me that she would be back. The car had still been running and the lights were on. I opened the door and got out, I needed some air, and I couldn't look at Pillz. She came back with two young Hispanic women in their early twenties. She told me to go with them, that she would take care of Kareem, that was what she called Pillz. I wiped the pound down and slid it into a sewer drain.

The two young women drove me all the way to New London, Connecticut which is on the other side of Rhode Island. They dropped me off at the bus station. I gave them three hundred dollars. They never asked me my name, and I did not ask them theirs. I bought a one-way ticket to NYC's 42nd St Bus Terminal. I had to get up out of New England. When I got on that bus about 6:30 in the morning, I went into the bathroom and cried for about half an hour. I had become an emotional wreck. Pillz was on my mind, Lisa had left her kids alone in the house to get us up out of there. She was hurting. I had killed again. I became nauseous at the thought of it. I was down a half a brick. All I did was lose on that trip, however it still was not enough to wake me up. Being stubborn or stupid I kept right at it. I had to regroup and think some things through.

A few things became very clear to me. There were people that would kill you anywhere. There were poor drug infested dangerous neighborhoods everywhere, my hood was not the only place that was like that. If I died or was incarcerated out of town away from the people who knew me; I would be on my own or a John Doe with no one to identify my corpse. It was standard procedure in the game that when you went out of town to do dirt that you had an alias. My name would no longer be Shamel I would become Peter, Ramel, J, Universal, or Refrigerator Head. It did not matter the name as long as it was not my real one. I generally picked names that did not raise an eyebrow or stand out. A veil of secrecy and anonymity was crucial in the game. I made it my business not to dress like my predecessors in the drug game.

I refused to wear heavy jewelry, that Mr. T look was not for me. I had developed two dress codes. One was a preppy look, I dressed as if I were going to school, casual. The second was I dressed in dark colored sweat pants or army fatigues with deep pockets that were suitable for collecting large amounts of money. While I was trapping, I always kept a black hoody. I liked the champion brand best, the material was thick, the hood could best conceal my face, and it was reminiscent of the grim reapers hood. The front pocket was spacious; I could keep a gun or drug package easily accessible when I needed to. I wore boots however generally they were not Timberlands. I liked Gortex best, the Vasquez type, they were more expensive than Timbs and better looking to me. They looked like a shoe/boot. I kept a Yankee fitted hat, it was a New York thing.

The more I had been exposed to made me aware of how naïve I had been, and that bothered me deeply at times. I realized how illogical and delusional I could be and how much I did not know or had not understood. For that reason, I always felt a little vulnerable and at risk of being rejected by life. The only remedy I had was to fear nothing but fear itself and ride the wave of blissful ignorance to its end. Due to that I lived a very uncertain and uncalculated life, that could only breed failure for me.

Out of town, New York was an army, we were seen as invaders. Coming to take over territory, money, and women. Generally, we were not welcomed. Three things typically kept us afloat and dominant: the drugs we supplied, our lack of hesitance to get violent namely shoot; and we were generally smart, charismatic, and diplomatic. I had to be that way, my survival depended on it.

When we were out of town people assumed two things about New York hustlers; one that we were all from NYC, and two that we were all from Brooklyn. Smart hustlers let the assumptions ride because the less they knew the better. Brooklyn was our designated hot representative. Remember what I said before, I was there for the fortune not the fame. As long as I was getting money, I could care less about who was from where. I had learned something else about myself. When it came down to it, I would bust my gun anywhere. I was not having it from anybody. It did not matter about culture, beliefs, or race. I just wanted to deal with real people and get rich. Everything else was red tape and rhetoric. I learned a few other things about the game and myself that I will discuss later.

I ended up in Binghamton, New York., it was a drug gold mine. It is located four hours from NYC in upstate New York. I earned my first one hundred thousand dollars out there. The drug clientele was predominantly white. I am talking ninety-nine percent. They wanted cocaine and heroin twenty-four hours a day nonstop. I had police, lawyers, doctors, clergy men, and business owners as my personal customers. They did not mind paying a little more for discretion and to keep their business private. At heart I had become a young business man. Confidentiality and respect became my main priorities with my customers and with people in general. Respect will always be the life blood of the streets. Lack of respect is why so many problems existed and continue to persist. I had never taken pride in beating on users, it was not my thing. I was more apt to treat them like family, after all my own mother and father were addicts. The few times I had to be aggressive with them, had to do with business.

There were addicts who were also hustlers. They would turn the houses they stayed in into drug stores, smoking, and shooting galleries; for users who had no place to get high or who would rather just get high there and keep spending money. I would give them g-packs which were fifty, twenty dollar stuffed small plastic bags of raw cocaine, the bag size was 5858. After they were stuffed and closed, they would be stapled shut, then the tip would be melted closed further with a lighter. This ensured that the bags were not tapped or that you knew if they were, because the seal would've been broken and could not be put back together again in the same way that it was originally. Customers who bought constantly knew that.

I made rounds to the spots every hour or so to make sure everything had been running smoothly. If a customer thought there was some funny business happening with the work; they would say something to me about it when they saw me. I encouraged that, it was customer service. If upon checking the work I determined it was tampered with, I would put hands on them violently. Subsequently made them work it off for free and pay back the customers whom they had cheated. It did not matter if they were White, Black, male, or female. If they played with the product, the money, or both they would definitely be slapped. It was equal rights, equal opportunity, and equal butt kicking.

At that time, I was part of a seven-man team, four Americans and three Jamaicans; we were all from Mount Vernon. We were all equal partners. We controlled five blocks, Liberty St, Munzel St, State St, Virgil St, and Country town which were small projects. We had eight spots within these blocks. We all had responsibilities: two bagged up work, two gunmen, two who distributed the work; and one who checked the spots, collected the money, and split the money up equally between us. We could have all done each other's jobs, however we elected to do it that way. I checked the spots, collected the money, and broke it down between us. I was the youngest and they all trusted me the most. I did not get high, smoke cigarettes, or drink. I was a sober soldier. Besides myself was Crime, Snake, Gunz, Cook, Shot, and Stacks our age range was from 15-22. We acquired the property by force and default.

Snake and I went out there with a guy named V. We were all from 3rd Ave, V had been part of a team of dudes from the heights part of Mt. Vernon, that had been getting money in Bing. They all worked for a dude named Water. V was not happy with the way he had been treated by Water, so he decided to break off and do his own thing. That was where Snake and I came in. The first trip went well. We took one hundred and twenty-five grams of raw cocaine, three guns, and some spending cash. It was the standard startup kit for me. If I had drugs to sell, guns for security, and money to spend I would set up shop; basically, anywhere provided it was worth my while and the reward outweighed the risk that I could see. You never really can tell which is more or less between risk and reward.

We sold off the work and were out of there in two days. V had a white crew out there that he had been running with: Katie, Paul, and Jimmy. It threw me off at first because I had never met white drug dealers before. Up until that point it had not occurred to me that they existed, but they had, and I was about to find out just how real they were. Katie had blonde hair and deep blue eyes. Paul had red hair and spotty freckles on his cheeks with light brown eyes. Jimmy had dark hair and brown eyes. All their parents were strung out on drugs, just like mine. Katie's mother turned tricks just to get high. They still sold drugs anyway and would do whatever it took to eat. Katie was V's girl and she did whatever he asked her to do. Paul and Jimmy had a local gang called the British Knights. They sold drugs, got high, and were violent. The police stayed on them, they were hot. I liked them, they just needed to calm down a bit, so they could really see some paper. I realized something about my generation which they were clearly in. What united us more than any religion or civil rights could; were drugs, music, poverty, and we all came from the same struggles.

We watched our parents abuse drugs and lose their self-respect, we went hungry and neglected emotionally because of it. Child abuse ran rampant, sexual abuse occurred for many. A white fiend named Maddy tried to sell me her newborn baby for some cocaine, she was dead serious. That was what type of vice grip drugs had on many. We could all relate to the hardcore lyrics of rap music. I am talking about street Hip Hop such as: NWA, Too Short, Tu-Pac, Snoop Dogg, NAS, Wu-Tang, Biggie Smallz, Jay Z,

Jadakiss, Styles P, Sheik Louch, Capone and Noriega, Mobb Deep, and DMX. On the flip side Stevie Wonder, Michael Jackson, Alicia Keys, and Beyoncé have also impacted the white mindset. When I hear white people use the word N****z or N*****s do I get upset? NO!

I used the word N**** and B**** all day even when I was around white people. They listened to the same music that I listened to that were saying those words every other sentence, and I was the Alpha, the dominant influence, why would I not expect them to mimic me? I hope you do not think Black people only mimic white people, for example exaggerated proper speech like you're from the valley when you are around your well to do educated white friends. I have learned that the Black thoughts and mindset have been just as impactful on the White mindset as the reverse has been true. I will come back to race relations shortly with a story to tell about it.

On the second and third trips things changed dramatically. The second trip V ran into Water his ex-boss. Water pulled out a gun on V and he ran. V was still in touch with most of Water's workers. They felt just like V. He did not pay them what they deserved, he talked disrespectfully to them, and he would sleep with their so-called girlfriends. V convinced them to flip on Water. We finished the work and went back to Mt Vernon. Snake and I went and bought more work. V told us to go back without him. He would be up there Sunday.

V and two of his mans that he got to flip and set Water up went to Connecticut; ran up in Water's Mother's home that he had bought her and where he laid low. They shot him to death while he was in the bed sleeping. They then began to scour the place for his money. They found seven hundred and fifty thousand dollars in a duffle bag and suit case right underneath the bed they had shot him on. What they did not realize is that his mother also laid in her bed in a different room and had called the police. As they exited the house, police ambushed them. I haven't seen V since then.

On the third trip out there, I met some other unfriendly New York drug dealers. We did not have much to worry about with the locals, but we did have to be concerned about other city dealers who were feeling very territorial. I had a baby face that had never been seen, standing in front of a trap house with Katie. He knew I was not from out there, he immediately pulled his J-30 over. I automatically gripped the 380 automatic I had in the pouch of my hoodie. He jumped out with heavy jewelry on. He was a short, fat, big belly fella, with gold teeth, and braids in his hair. I thought quick, I had to outsmart this joker. He was either blinded by his ego and perception of me or did not have any real sense of safety, because he was about to get popped. I had already seen it in my mind. All I had to do was brandish the gun, shoot him, and he would be done.

I really desired to stay out there and get money, so I thought twice about shooting him. Even if I hit him and got away, I would still lose, I would not have made the money that I came for, because I would have to leave. I decided to entertain his theatrics down to the last second to see what the result would be. I would not jump out of the window and just start firing on him; instead I waited patiently. He asked me," who are you out here with?' I said, "nobody, I am by myself chilling with shorty." He said, "what up" to her, they knew each other. He said, "you cannot be up here." I said, "there is enough money for both of us." He said, "no there is not. I do not care if I go to Japan for fifty years, I do not want you out here, this is private property.

Do you understand me?"

I really wanted to do something to him, but I kept the bigger objectives in mind. I simply said, "Aight." He smirked at Katie like he had the biggest balls in the world after that slick talk that I seemed to be submissive too. I swear I really wanted to laugh but maintained my façade. Then he put the cherry on top when he turned back to me and said, "I will be back in twenty minutes and I do not want to see you out here when I return. If you need a ride to the bus station let me know and I will call a cab." I said "Nah, I'm good, I'll be out of here." He just turned and waddled back to his car.

I had learned that you do not offend someone and then turn your back on them, but he did just that. He had a nice car, but he clearly was an amateur, whom was fast asleep. Before he even hopped back in the car, I asked her does she know where he be at, she told me to ask Paul.

Paul murdered the bozo for me. I had the local gangstas with me, Water was gone, V was gone, there were a few other city boys out there, but they stayed in their lane and opted not to make it any hotter than it was. After all they were there for the money too. Bozo had four young boys up there with him. Two went back to the city, one started smoking crack, and the other one had two white baby mamas out there and faded to black. Back then that was the movement for a lot of so-called bosses. Many of those would be chiefs would go get some hungry young boys and girls to bully. Put them in the spot, feed them, and buy them outfits every now and again.

I was glad my predecessors had not raised me or treated me like that. My older counterparts treated me as an equal because I pulled my weight and then some. They showed me how to be a trustworthy man in the street game, also to be responsible. After that incident we set up shop. It was Snake's idea to go get reinforcements. This was where our seven-man crew came in. He said we needed to organize the set up a little better. I went with his flow to see his vision. I was curious and still young with a lot to learn. My personal thought was that I could be alright just with the local crew, they did not mind putting in work, they had demonstrated trust and loyalty. They were ready to get money, and we got along great. There was not a spec of tension between us.

They came up, things were good for about eighteen months, then the empire started falling apart. Like they say all good things must come to an end. Jimmy killed a police officer, then was killed by one. Paul got twenty years for Arson. He had set fire to a hotel, with one fatality, and multiple injuries. Katie started sleeping with Crime, they both had started sniffing dope. They all started stealing from the money we made together, before I could break it down properly. They had intercepted the cash pickups I would make, by going to get the money first. They would also find the money I stashed around the house we shared and started spending that. I am talking about unanswered missing thousands of dollars a day, every day.

We went from getting 10 kilos to buying 2 amongst 7 of us. Gunz and Cook fell out over some Jamaican beef they had that I did not get into or care to understand. One's family member was Shower Posse and the other was a Spanglas or something to that effect, those were Jamaican gang slash political parties. Cook ended up killing Gunz over that irreconcilable difference. Shot and Stacks started robbing all the other city drug dealers out there. Three months after my sixteenth birthday, Snake and I got knocked with a kilo on route 17 in the town of Monroe and were sent to Orange County jail. Snake and I were not alone in the car. I will start that story on race, I promised now.

Snake and I needed to make a quick trip to Manhattan to pick up some fish scale. My connect called me and let me know that he had one brick of raw left. If I wanted it, I had to come right away because he was getting ready to fly out of town and a drought was about to happen. Crime and Katie were missing with the Pathfinder; Black and Shot had the Benz with the stash box in it that we would have Katie drive to go pick up work in. Our community and empire would not stop falling apart.

There had been a guy named Billy that I had met when I first landed in Binghamton. We had a little history and a great rapport. Billy was a redneck, a full-blooded strawberry blonde haired, blue eyed, white man about forty years old. He was also a cocaine using heroin addict. He liked to speed ball, which is when an addict shoots up heroin with a needle and then when the high goes down, they shoot up some cocaine to bring the high back up. Heroin is a downer and cocaine is the upper.

Billy came through the block in his white pickup truck with the confederate flag on his license plate bracket. He drove through the block screaming, "Yeeeee-Hawwwww!" Like he was one of the Dukes of Hazard. I got a kick out of it. It was beyond hilarious to me. He may have been a white supremacist, but when he came to see me, the dope had become supreme: and I became the God who gave him supremacy. You could travel so far upstate that you would think you were in the deep south in some parts, especially with the KKK. I had been fortunate that I had not experienced blatant racism yet, or maybe I had.

On that day Billy came through in a 4-door gray Ford Taurus with his girlfriend to score. You can call it perfect timing because I was making my last round at that spot. I propositioned him with money and drugs for his service. We went and picked Snake up and left for the city. We went down there handled our business and were on our way back when the worst happened. We were stopped by NYS Troopers. We were travelling on Route 17 North and had just passed through a toll booth not far from the Woodbury Common Outlets. Upon coming out of the tollbooth area Billy steered the Taurus into one of the oncoming highway lanes. I had my eyes closed semi sleep in the backseat behind Billy, while Snake sat next to me, behind Amy. I do not know if Billy put the signal on before he started to guide us into a lane. We were pulled over for allegedly changing lanes without using the signal, otherwise known as swerving.

Once the lights on the Trooper's Police Car were activated behind us, the atmosphere inside our car changed. I shook whatever sleep I had on me off. Snake appeared to be sobering up. He had been smoking a blunt and had just finished it moments before we pulled up to the toll booth. Amy was up front in the passenger seat putting on her seatbelt, as Billy was with his. Billy navigated the car for about another mile before he decided to pull onto the shoulder of the road. Before he shouldered it, he made a few statements to us. First, he said he did not have his driver's license, he also let us know the car was not registered. I felt sick to my stomach. Snake said to him that if they searched the car, he had to hold that down. Amy started to say something, Billy cut her off and said, "alright just make sure Amy gets home." I assured him that if the worst happened, that I would take care of him; he trusted and believed me.

When the worst happened, I kept my word. When we finally pulled over in the town of

Monroe, the trooper ordered the driver to turn the vehicle off over the PA system of his cruiser. To the troopers who approached the car we must've looked like we were from two different worlds. Billy and Amy represented one world in the front seat; Snake and I another in the back seat. Musically they were country and we were hip hop. They were older white people with a grungy look, and we were young Black teenage boys who looked well-kept and very clean. Their suspicions of it had to be high, because after Billy told the trooper that he did not have a license or registration, he ordered him out of the car, cuffed him, then escorted him back to his cruiser. Within a minute of that, another cruiser pulled up behind the first one then we were all in handcuffs.

Amy, Snake, and I stood on the side of the road in the warm spring night air as vehicles flew by and the troopers ransacked the car, we were just sitting in cuffs until they found the mother load. They discovered one thousand grams of cocaine and about one hundred syringes, we had just bought as well. We sold needles to heroin addicts because they always asked for them to shoot up with. The troopers acted as if they found the leprechaun's gold at the end of the rainbow, that was big for them. We were all transported to the state trooper barracks. Billy took the charge, he claimed the kilo, and did not waiver even when a trooper told him to just say that it had belonged to Snake and I. They let us out, we were in the middle of nowhere. I had fourteen hundred dollars in my pocket and Snake had some money. We had put Amy in a cab back to Binghamton after we got her information, then we took a cab back to Mt. Vernon.

I retained and paid for an attorney to represent Billy. I sent him some money and I even bought Amy a RX7 two door sports car, so she could drive down and see Billy two hours away in Orange County. I also kept her high on heroin basically for free. We all had a bond and it did not matter that they were white hillbillies and addicts, or that we were Black urban drug dealers. They had kept it tall with us, they had not snitched us out.

Billy ended up getting thirty-six months at a treatment center with no prison time. The cocaine laws were not as harsh as crack laws. We had gotten busted with the raw cocaine and Billy was a white male with a drug problem, who had never been arrested. They were lenient with him. Amy even decided to check into rehab, which I helped her with. Life had become more complex for me with its irony and contradictions. Things were not what they had always appeared to be. At times what appeared to be opposites were the same, and what appeared to be the same were opposites.

I had not stopped hustling. I ran the same route up and down 17. I had become more conscious of the consequences, but I kept dealing. The more I had to lose, the higher up I went in the drug game; the more deceptive I became. When I had two grams on the corner selling, everybody could find me and knew my business. Now that I had two kilos, I had become hard to find and only an elite few knew what I was doing or how I was moving. That was what the smartest dealers in the game did, blend in, be inconspicuous., stay low under the radar, and stick to the business. I funded ambitious hustlers that I believed in, male and female with money, guns; and drugs when they needed to make moves to other towns, cities, or states. It was all an investment. Some investments were successful, and others were not. If you made money and thrived you were successful, if you went to jail, were robbed, or killed then you were unsuccessful. I never made any legal business investments. The truth was I didn't know how to, nor did I think in that capacity.

My mother and father were strung out on drugs and I had no one I could trust with the type of money I had been earning. I buried money, left it in locked lockers at the bus station, and spent it recklessly. I paid for several apartments and cars none of which were in my name. I was generous with females I dealt with and generous to some of my family members. My sisters and brothers were too young to handle business, and they had started to get into trouble in the streets. I had money, but I did not know how to take it to the next level and become legit. I had no one to show me how, so I got stuck in the trap.

Two things happened that changed life once again for me. I had been on my way to Binghamton when Katie called me on my cell phone and informed me the Feds and DEA were out there and had raided everything and arrested everybody. She told me not to come there. That was the last time I spoke to Katie. She too was detained by the Feds sometime after that. I made a U-turn somewhere right outside Monticello, NY on the highway and threw my cell phone out of the window. I have never been back to Bing since. I had a large sum of money and drugs out there that I had to charge to the game. The second thing that happened was Snake got shot multiple times in a botched robbery attempt. He laid silent in a coma for over a month. I found out who did it to him and retaliated. There were two of them, Turtle and Greazy. I gunned them down at a dice game they were at, Greazy lived and Turtle died.

Greazy gave a statement saying I had been the shooter who shot them both, and that I was Snake's friend, he would know where to find me.

Detectives went to Snake who had just been released from the hospital. They pressed him about me and my whereabouts. He told them where my mother and father lived, and where two of my stash spots might be located. They hit all four spots. I was not in any of them. When I found out that Snake had led the police to these places, I felt betrayed. I honestly did not know what to do. I was heartbroken, bitter, desensitized, and lost without direction.

The whole way of life I had been living had been worth nothing. Most of the friendships that I thought I had were not genuine. The money I had been making was easy come, easy go, and it did not matter how much it had been. I had killed people for loyalties that did not really exist. At the core of myself, I had become deeply unsatisfied and unhappy with who I had become as a person. I had not been the loving, kind, compassionate, empathetic person that I naturally was and desired to be. The way I demonstrated my love for someone could mean death to the person who hurt them. My life had spiraled completely out of control. I would never fully be seen in the way that I really was and wanted to be known. Instead I would be known and perceived as a drug dealer, robber, and murderer.

I turned myself in, not out of fear, because only a scared man would keep running. At that point I feared nothing but fear itself. Equally, whatever infatuation, need, fantasy, or hope I may have had about being a drug lord or living life as an outlaw dried up. The truth was, I felt all alone. There was no happy ending to the life I had been living. I was ready to face whoever and whatever, no matter the consequences, but I would not live in hiding. To keep killing at that point, seemed senseless to me. Wanting to protect myself, wanting to protect my family, wanting to protect my friends, wanting to protect my interests, my wanting to be taken seriously, my distrust for police, my inner anger, peer pressure, ignorance, my household, my neighborhood, my environment, my feelings of vulnerability, my feelings of helplessness, my feelings of uncertainty, my need to belong to fit in, my lack of education, my lack of understanding, my lack of positive guidance, and my choice to be a predator instead of being the prey had helped bring me to the crossroad I was now standing at.

When I look back hindsight being 20/20, and reflect I think I had been suffering from Post-Traumatic Stress Disorder or PTSD. It is a mental health condition triggered by experiencing or seeing a terrifying event. It is very common. There are more than 3 million documented cases per year. Imagine how many cases go undetected or undocumented due to poverty because poor people cannot afford to obtain the help they may need to be diagnosed. PTSD cannot be cured, but treatment may help. It is also chronic, which means it can last for months, years, or be lifelong with the triggers that can bring back memories of the trauma accompanied by intense emotional and physical reactions. Symptoms include flashbacks, nightmares, and anxiety. I had experienced many terrifying events. A person could be affected by the disorder as early as three years old and every age group older than that can be affected.

In the end it did not matter if I had been consumed with mental issues related to PTSD or not. The judge sentenced me to 40 years to life for my actions of murder and attempted murder on Turtle and Greazy The evidence that would be the nail in the coffin came from Greazy. Simply stated, he got on the stand pointed at me and said I did it.

Greazy had a reputation as a bonafide thug

who kept his business in the street, but not this time, his business would be handled in the courtroom. To be honest a part of me did not believe Greazy would take the stand, but he did. At that point I had become too desensitized to feel anything.

Instead of worrying about the time I had been sentenced to exclusively, I made a conscious decision to get to know myself in every way I possibly could. I needed to know why I did what I did. Namely why did I think the way I thought. I would become my own behavioral scientist and study myself. Observe those around me more consciously. I underestimated the magnitude of that task, because it was and continues to be a serious challenge.

What raised the difficulty level of that challenge was entering New York State Department of Corrections. It would be a new world to me that I would have to be born into because I knew nothing about it. I was packed up and transported from Westchester County Jail, Valhalla, to Downstate Correctional Facility, on a cold January morning. I was twenty years old with a 40-year sentence. I had to do twice as much time as I had been alive, before I could even be eligible for parole. Even then my freedom would not be certain, because I had life on the back of that. Besides getting to know myself, I gave myself rules that I would live and die by in prison.

First, I would not become homosexual in any way. Second, I would never be a snitch, if I had a problem, I would handle it. Third, I would not turn to drugs heroin, crack, cocaine, weed, nor psychiatric medication. Psychiatric meds were known as liquid handcuffs, because once the liquid cuffs were on your mind, they would not need to physically handcuff your wrists. I needed to be conscious and aware of what I was always thinking and feeling. Fourth, I would not commit suicide. I felt that would be weak and beneath who I really was, I still feel that way. Fifth, I would stay G'd up, meaning I would remain a 100% real man that would not be bullied and not seek to bully others either. Sixth, I would move with respect. I would give it and expect it in return, as I always had. Respect has been and always will be very important to me. I do not have to trust you or love you, but I will respect you. It is a common courtesy. With respect as a base any type of positive growth is possible. Seventh, discipline would be my comfort zone it would be the zone from which I studied, learned, and developed self-control to be a better person. Eighth, I would never stop learning, because I had too much to learn and I knew very little. I would respect education as I had always. Ninth, I would get in shape and stay healthy. It was my life, I had to take care of it.

Tenth, I would stay clean. I would continue to bathe, groom myself, wash my clothes, and brush my teeth. I would not let myself go, I would not fall apart. Eleventh, I would still reach out to my daughter and let her know that she had a father who loved her. To this point in the story I have not mentioned her, I will explain why later. Twelfth, I would always love my family. It did not matter how dysfunctional we were, and even though they could do nothing for me. These were some of the ground rules I set for myself upon entering DOC, now it is time to Enter DOC.

DeShawn Kenner

Part Two:

Department of

Corrections

DeShawn Kenner

Welcome to the DOC

The Department of Corrections is the third part of the criminal justice system. The criminal justice system has three main parts. First there is the police, the ones that arrest you. Second is the court system, the judges, prosecutors, and defense attorneys. That is where you are tried, convicted, sentenced, or released. The Westchester County Correctional Officers transferred custody of me to the Downstate Maximum-Security Correctional Facility. I was then considered state property. I had realized something about the DOC as a whole, on the county and state level, they both sought to correct you by brute force and instilled fear.

Intimidation defined the style of how they would be correcting the incarcerated. I saw the flaws in DOC immediately. I could not be corrected for the better through violence, fear, or intimidation. That type of anxiety in the community I had grown up in had already helped to harden me, desensitize me, and made me violent. Coming into DOC made it apparent to me any changes made had to be intrinsically existential. Nevertheless, I learned how to play their game.

I was reintroduced to more traumatic stress. It could not be considered post-traumatic stress, because it had only just begun. The officers made it clear from the very beginning that we were enemies. We were not friends; we would never be friends. They did not trust us, respect us, or care about us at all. Oddly enough that attitude was not new to me. Long before I committed any crime, police had already made me feel that way. On either side of the wall my enemies remained the same: law enforcement, my own kind, and my own self. I had to make peace with myself first and then seek peace with the others, if possible. I wondered if the police and DOC had me labeled as the enemy, how could the court system be any different? Was there really balance between the two or just one in the same?

Upon arrival to Downstate, the officers waited until we were all unlocked and moved from transport vehicles into one big bull pen. They then entered the bull pen about twenty deep with their batons out and gave us a speech that started something like, 'this is not Rikers Island, Valhalla, Long Island, or anywhere else you may have come from, you are now in state custody.'

I had been given a din number which consisted of six numbers and one letter, it was like my new social security number. It validated who I was while incarcerated. I also received a baldy haircut, a cold shower, state green pants & shirts, a pair of black state boots, a pair of white state sneakers, under clothes, and bed linens.

Next, I and several other newly convicted felons were escorted to our cells in a building in 2 complex. I went into 14 cell and the door slammed behind me. We were an assorted group of guys from different areas and jails. Regardless of where we came from, we were all the same to them, state property.

We were allowed one five-minute phone call per week while in downstate. I called no one, there was no one to call, I was on my own. My mother and father were still more concerned with getting high, than they were about me. Everyone I had sold drugs with in the streets stayed away; they were still in the game and I understood that. They did not want me to make them hot with police, nor did I want them to ever be able to say that I brought the police to them. It was just that simple, everybody kept it moving. There was no real love in the streets. Everything had been based on what you could do for the next man.

Snake ran with his former enemies and life went on. I had been loyal to a fault. Most of the problems I had when it ended in violence, stemmed from one of my so-called friends. I made their problems, my problems. I prided myself on standing up for those that were with me or around me. Even if they wouldn't do the same for me, a part of me felt like a fool.

The money I made had become a gift to anybody who found it or still owed it to me. Honestly, I exercised poor money management and for that I had nothing to show. Even if I had a few thousand dollars that came to me via money order, it was still a drop in the bucket compared to what I had earned over the years. Drug dealing had been my full-time job. I risked a lot. I should've had more but I did not. I had not put it in banks, I could not trust anyone with it, and I could not take it with me.

I had put myself in this nasty situation with

no one to blame, but me. I had elected myself to be Snake's protector and avenger. Even though he and I were close, he had not asked me to do what I did. It was my way of showing love and loyalty to him. That was the code I had chosen to live my life by in the streets. Anytime I had pulled the trigger I used my own finger and no one else's. I had been responsible for my life's outcomes for better or worse. Even if the police and CO's were out to get me all I had ever done was add fuel to the fire. The most I could do was stay as far away from them as possible and hoped for the best.

Racism

Honestly, I had never experienced blatant racism until I came into the department of corrections. It seemed to me that the white officers were really comfortable with their bigotry and hatred for Black prisoners. I had heard young White boys like Jimmy and Paul use the word n**** and it did not bother me because they followed behind myself and rap music. They even referred to one another as n****s. From those mainly middle aged, out of shape, tattooed, White officers it came from a different place. The intonations from them were more Klan like.

I just soaked it all up, I did not get emotional about it. Part of me had been amused because I had never witnessed any type of officer use the word n****. That bigotry would be in every maximum-security prison I would be transferred to; it was the norm. Until that point only White people's actions had expressed the word, not their mouths. Another racial slur that I found intriguing was crack baby. At times there even Black officers around, and they said nothing. Truth be told many of them were just as bad and at times worse. Many of them even viewed us as savages.

Ticket System

In addition to governing by force and fear officers were encouraged to write tickets that cost inmates $5 each. Getting a ticket meant that you had broken a rule set by DOC. They were just about impossible to beat. Nine times out of ten, if you had gotten a ticket, you would be found guilty. Not only would you have to pay $5 for getting the ticket, you would also be locked in your cell, or sent to the Special Housing Unit (SHU aka box), for a designated period of time. There were other privileges that could've been suspended such as: commissary; recreation which meant no fresh air, exercise, or phone; and suspended visits which meant you would see no one but an attorney. Sentences were passed down by prison Sergeants, Lieutenants, Captains, or some other high-ranking prison civilian. Their non-ranking officers wrote most of the tickets and the high-ranking officers pretended to be empathetic, fair, and impartial judges at your hearing. The system was fixed.

There were two tickets that typically could never be beaten. One for direct orders, which meant that if a CO told you to do something you had to do it immediately. The other for harassment, if a CO said you harassed them you would be disciplined. It was always their word against yours at the hearing in front of their superiors. Your word had not meant spit and the money made from writing tickets went toward amenities they could enjoy. Even if by chance you were lucky enough to beat a ticket, you still never got your $5 back.

Writing tickets was a multi-million-dollar big business scheme. I understood the need to be skeptical or doubt many of the tickets that were written against inmates. What would prevent them from embellishing? Who could stop them?

There had been no checks and balances.

It was well known and understood that if you caught a ticket it would be in your best interest to plead guilty, because it would lessen the penalty that you were bound to get. Pleading guilty meant the difference of being keep-lock for 7 days or going to the SHU for 7 months if you tried to fight a ticket to the very end. It was a lose-lose, or the lesser of two evils situation. I had learned not to knock the hustle, but it bothered me that I had become part of the hustle of DOC. Despite having known all of this I still took high risks and plenty of them.

About My Love Life

The first time I hooked up with a girl sexually I was fourteen years old. I had not known her, nor had she known me personally before our encounter. She knew me vicariously through some mutual friends whom I was popular with. They all went to private school together, one of those Blessed Sacrament Sacred Heart Catholic Schools. They had a house party and our mutual friends invited me. I had gone with my boy Devin. The party was in the Bronx. As soon as we went through the door it was lit. There were a bunch of half-naked teenage girls and guys in the place. They had liquor and weed but I did not drink or smoke.

I was introduced to everyone; it was all love. As soon as I removed my coat and took a seat, a pretty, young thing jumped right in my lap. She was not shy at all and clearly staked her claim and marked her territory. Her name was Marisol. She was Columbian, and the party was at her house. After that everyone started dipping off into different rooms and corners. We stayed in the room we were in. She stepped out of her booty cut sweat shorts and took off her t-shirt, but she still had her bra on. She had a beautifully cinnamon toned athletic body. We were the same age, however she seemed way more advanced with this than me, because I had not known what to do. All I knew was that she had aroused me. She rolled out a blanket over the carpet, dimmed the lights more, and then laid back on it. Instinctively I took off my clothes and went to her. I hovered above her as she laid on her back. I had become fully erect. She grabbed my erection and guided it inside of her and the rest was history. The sensation of pleasure that I felt had overwhelmed me, and I released it inside of her. In less than a minute, my first time had come to an end. I went to the bathroom and examined the natural juices that my private parts were soaked in. I touched it, smelled it, and looked at it before I had washed it away, with some warm water and soap that had been sitting in a dish on the bathroom sink. I had been standing in front of the mirror to see if I looked any different, now that I was no longer a virgin. Nothing had changed, I looked the same.

I strolled out of the bathroom back to her. We went at it all night after that, with no condoms or cares. I had known it was reckless, but at the time I knew nothing about safe sex. No one had ever discussed that topic with me. Fortunately for the both of us nothing bad came out of our one-night stand. Since then many lovers have come and gone out of my life, but I have never known real love.

I had no high school sweetheart, I did not even finish high school. My relationships were based on lust, money, or street reputation. Either the female lusted me because: I was handsome and young, they wanted to get some money out of me, because I had been getting money; or because I had earned a reputation as a hot boy, gangsta, or real n****. I was shooting, stabbing, and getting money. I must admit that I had not put much effort in to getting to know the females I had been with either. I had not really known how to get to know a female. I had not had the time to get to know a female, nor had the patience for most of the females I had been with.

After my first sexual experience my mentality had set in that females either wanted to do it or not, but I would not waste a tremendous amount of time waiting to find out. We had not needed to do much talking. Next, I had been moving weight, selling drugs, and that was a full-time responsibility. I had to get the work, move the work, stash the work, bag the work, sell the work, worry about the cops, worry about would-be stick up kids, I had to get the money, and stash the money. I had to re-up workers and I would be in and out of town with it constantly. I would stay where I was at until I was done doing what I had to do. I stayed on the low. I had become very hard to find, especially if you were not in line with what I was doing.

I had slept with women that were convenient for me. I would just bag them wherever I was at or had to be. It had become a calculated thing with me, that I based on their necessity to my causes. Maybe she had a place to get low in, a car to switch up in, or be a drug mule for me amongst other things. There had to be a purpose that was typically bigger than sex. I could get that anywhere.

She had not needed to be the baddest chick. Speaking of which I had some really physically beautiful females that I wish it could've worked out with. One of three things always seemed to happen that neither one of us would tolerate, mainly me though. They either had attitudes that I would not deal with, they wanted more time than I could give them, or they started demanding more money once they were sure I had it. That was a major turn off for me. We had let money come between us. I did not mind taking care of anybody who was with me or in my corner, but when they started acting like I owed them, it made me look at them differently. I had done things because I wanted to do them, not because someone said do them or else. I was not married to any of them and I had not had children with any of them. Even if I had I still was not having it, I believed a female who truly loved me would not come at me sideways for my bread, nor would consciously try to get on my nerves or underneath my skin. It had not mattered how gorgeous or sexy she was, a nasty attitude and a poor personality were deal breakers for me. It literally was like sleeping with the enemy for me.

When I was nineteen years old, a young woman named Norkel gave birth to our daughter. I was there for the birth and cut the umbilical cord. We named her Maya. Norkel was a hustler like me. That was how we hooked up, in the dope game. We had always been around each other, the chemistry sparked between us and one thing led to another like a touch to a kiss. She looked impressive to my eye. She was not model pretty, more like the girl next door attractive. Beside her being down to earth and funny, I did not have to hide who I was or what I had been into from her. She knew what time it was with me, and I with her. We smoked weed, drank liquor together, then had sex like wild animals in the jungle.

After having Maya, Norkel had a change in

her heart and way of thinking. She wanted to stop selling drugs and she wanted me to stop too. Since she had become a mother everything was too dangerous for her. I understood her point of view; however, I was not prepared to make that change. It had become a habit that I could not break that easily nor was willing to do so. I had been selling drugs since I was thirteen or fourteen years old nonstop. How could I have just given it up? The drug game had brought us together, supported our lavish lifestyles, and our child was the divine product of that. Why could I have not been a great daddy and a drug dealer?

I had bought that little girl everything she needed and then some. That had not been enough to satisfy Kel's concerns, she took our daughter and moved back down south where she was originally from. I had just let them go. She had made her own money; she hadn't needed me. Nonetheless I wanted to be a father to my child.

She had brought Maya home to her family for the first time. I visited them a couple of times. I had been introduced to her mother, father, sisters, brothers, grandparents, cousins, and friends. It seemed like everybody in her town was somehow related. She was part of a big family.

A few of her cousins that I had met were local dope boys. They had pumped their drugs out of shotgun houses, those were one story houses you could walk all the way from the front door straight through out of the backdoor, or they sold out of the yard. Trappin' and trap houses were everywhere and came in different styles depending on the region you were in. You could turn any home into a trap house just by selling drugs out of it. It did not matter if it was a building, a bungalow, a townhouse, a family home, a shotgun house, a street corner, a hotel, or a yard as long as it had become a place where you could buy drugs; it became a trap or a spot.

Some hustlers had even delivered it to your door, providing door to door service, as at times I had.

Norkel and I had been friends at a minimum. Her cousins and I discussed making a drug investment together. She had found out about it and asked me not to do it. She had not wanted me to bring my drug game or expertise out there. She had really started getting on my nerves with her anti-selling drugs campaign for me. I needed to be close to our daughter and I needed to continue doing what I had been doing. It would have been a win-win for me.

Reluctantly I complied with her request. I let the boys know that it was not personal, but I was falling back from our plan. I had done them a favor, before I left some dudes had come up from Miami and set up shop. They had been aggressive with the boys. I shut it down for them and then I bounced. Norkel was upset about that. Everything I had done became a problem for her now. Her attitude bothered me because she had known what time it was with me from day one and had been cool with it. Then she was always nervous, complaining, and accusing me of not caring about my child. She made a whole one hundred and eighty degrees turn and was completely different than when we had met.

While I had still been in reception at Downstate Norkel sent me a letter that basically said.

"Hey, how are you? You are a good dude, but you did not listen to me when I asked you to stop doing what you were into, you had your chance. If you need something let me know, but I am not doing all this time with you. You got life! That is too much. Also, I met somebody, and I love him with every part of me. I am 8 months pregnant with his baby. You had your chance, now it is my turn. - Kel…PS your daughter will always know that you are her daddy."

I was not mad at her or anyone else for that matter who would go on in life, without me. I had come to the understanding with myself that nobody owed me anything. I had made my decisions, did things my way, and whatever was owed to me, I would charge to the game. After all, they had been my choices, so they equally were my consequences. I blamed no one for what I had done. I took responsibility for my actions, if only to myself, it gave me a sense of peace.

I asked Kels to make sure our daughter was safe, that she knew I loved her, to send me some pictures of our daughter every now and then, and if any of my family wanted to meet her, that she would make that happen. I asked her for nothing else. Kels had always honored my request, that was love to me. I had been accustomed to that type of love and learned to expect it as such.

Accepting My Circumstances

I focused on adjusting to life in prison. There had been a great deal to learn about it because I knew nothing at all. I had never been to prison before. I never even visited someone, and I knew lots of people locked up, both males and females. Some of which I had made money with. The game always went on, so I already had known not to expect it to stop for me either. I had not expected many visits from it. Besides I had acquired many aliases in the streets. Anywhere I had drifted to I came up with a new nickname. I took the precautionary measure just in case I had gotten hot or had made it hot. Mostly none of the acquaintances I had made in the street knew my government name or where I stayed. Many had not even known where I was from. After a while in the game my aim had been just to blend in and not be known. Concealing my identity had been very important to me. I left the scene quietly, to many of my acquaintances I simply disappeared. They had no idea where I went. Either way I had planned on disappearing, but not in the manner that I had. I had originally envisioned myself disappearing into the lap of luxury; compliments of the drug game and the work I had put in for it. It had not happened how I planned, and I failed to plan for anything else.

I had gotten a visit once while I was in Downstate. My sister Shawnika came to see me. She brought her baby son with her to see me. My nephew was only one-year-old; it was good to see them. I never missed them more than I did in that moment. She had put on some weight. She told me I had lost too much weight and looked bad. I thought I looked slim and fit. I guess I had over done it in her eyes. I had a distorted view of myself. The mirrors we were allowed were four by six-inch plastic fun house style or eight by ten-inch fiber glass style that enlarged everything like a magnifying glass. I had learned over the years I had many distorted views. I had been caught in the matrix and had not even known it. At least now I know.

Shawnika had married her puppy love boyfriend. We had all grown up together on the same block. Victor was like family already. He had always treated her right; he was a stand-up dude. They had kept each other out of trouble, they both had been going down the wrong road for a minute. I was happy for them. Shawnika had ended up in Spotford Detention for Youth for assault and robbery. Her crew of girlfriends and herself started fighting with some girls at Skate Key in the Bronx. They ended up taking their jewelry, money, and whatever else they decided to take. She and her cohorts were arrested for that. Luckily, she only ended up taking a program in a building in Harlem on 125th

St. Her record had been sealed as a youthful offender. Victor had been in the streets; he wasn't too far from the road I was on. I believe he had gotten caught making a drug sale. He had been put on house arrest. His record had also been sealed as a youthful offender. They helped keep each other focused. They held me down when they could with what I needed; mainly with money, phone calls, food packages, and checking in on my daughter.

Settling into Max Life

I was packed up and sent to Great Meadows also known as Comstock. It's another maximum-security prison with a tall thick concrete wall around it. Just about all the old maximums have walls around them. I had not stayed there long, and I learned a lot in my short stay. Comstock taught me that it was not what you saw in prison that you should be worried about, but what you didn't see that was dangerous. Although I had just come to prison, I had a crew and was gangbangin'.

I had become involved with a gang by way of some other gangstas. They embraced me, and I decided to roll with the rush. We had large numbers in the yard with weapons and all of that, but that had not curved the determination of one lone wolf. Metaphorically speaking, I fell asleep in the yard. After coming out and spinning the yard several hundred times looking for enemies that I had known of or would be enemies that might've wanted some static and finding none I could see, I relaxed a little bit. That was where I went wrong.

Turtle had an older brother there who had been locked up ten years already. He got wind of who I was just by dudes shouting me out and saying my name. He put together who I was. In prison social status became your wealth. It would take you further than money a lot of times. My name was solid, I shot right up in the elite class of prisoners. I was not a snitch, I was a killer, I had been a hustler who moved weight, and I had the paperwork to prove it. Not to mention the real n****s that had vouched for me.

When I had gone to trial, I learned the FBI had been trying to put a case together against me since I had been picked up with Snake, Amy, and Billy. That was something else that I had not seen but had happened. They had given me the paperwork at my Sandoval hearings. I had been labeled official, but I was not the only official dude behind the wall. Nor was the only one who would seek revenge. I still had to build my reputation here. I was watching TV in the yard with my hands in my pockets sitting on the bleachers when it happened. I had become way too comfortable.

It was close to eight o'clock in the evening, Big B had come to get me. It was time to go into the weight pile to workout. B was my age, he was from Bed Stuy, and he had a homicide like myself. He had twenty-five to life. We met in Downstate and got tight over the year we were there. Now we were here, and we would hold each other down. They sold thirteen inch black and white TV's on commissary, however my money had not gotten to this place yet from Downstate. I had not even gotten to go to commissary yet. Commissary was the store for prisoners where you bought: food, drinks, hot pots, TVs, radios, soup, deodorant, stamps, paper, pens, and other things provided you had the money. I opted to keep watching TV. He left with someone else to go workout. I looked behind me with my hands still in my pockets to see who was there.

No one had been in my immediate circumference except for an old timer sitting on the same bleacher as myself, just a little further down towards the end. The funny thing was I saw the guy walking my way at a close distance, but I had dismissed his relevance. I had seen him a couple of times before the incident. Straight up he was no match for me at all. He was about five feet five inches tall, weighed one hundred thirty pounds soaking wet, and not in shape at all. I was six feet tall, one hundred ninety-five pounds, charged up with muscle. I had been looking for some action.

He walked right up behind me. I must have been sitting at the perfect height for him to do his work. Almost as if I had been in a barber's chair, and he was the barber. He made his incision so gently that I had not even felt it. It had been breezy and a little chilly out there. I mistook his touch for light wind or maybe I thought B had come back and was playing around. Either way I had not budged as he attempted to send me out of life. I was like the perfect sacrifice. I sat there perfectly still, looking too focused on the TV screen. I made it easy for him. It was not until the old timer next to me on the bench said something that I realized what had been going on. He said, "youngblood I think he just tried to cut your throat."

I had immediately run my fingers across my neck but there had been no blood. I sprang onto my feet in attack mode. I turned and saw him looking back at me. We locked stares, he started running. I chased him around the large concrete parking lot looking yard. He had run in the direction of two CO's. They had stopped him, I walked the other way. They put a floodlight on me, four officers had run my way. One of them handcuffed my hands behind my back and walked me through the gate and out of the yard. We made it to the hallway.

To them I seemed like the aggressor, so before I was uncuffed, a sergeant said to me, "when we uncuff you, if you do anything to one of my officers, we will kill you." I had not taken his threat seriously for two reasons. First, I was not afraid and second, I had not planned on doing anything to them. I actually thought he was weird, because I had not understood where the remark had come from. I had to remember we were deemed natural enemies over everything else. I was more disappointed in the fact that I had gotten caught slipping. There I was, an enemy just tried to kill me and the other ones that had me cuffed told me that they would kill me. If I could have gotten my hands on a gun right then, I would have murdered them all.

That had been my wake-up call, my prison christening. I ended up getting twenty stitches across my neck that left a three-and-a-half-inch scar. He had cut me; however, it had not been deep enough to finish the job. I had become a victim of my own violence. I told them I had not known who did it, they let him go. I may have been caught slipping, but I would not be labeled a snitch. Anyone could get caught slipping but how you responded to it defined who you were. First, I went to face him, and he ran, he was a coward. Second, I had not cared if he wanted them to know he did it or not, I would never point the finger at him. I would have rather died first. I had been in the game long enough and had done enough dirt to know that you couldn't always win. I just strived to win more than I lost so when I had lost, I lost big. After that incident, I was keep locked for ninety days and involuntarily segregated, because they had not known who did that to me and I would not talk. I cut everybody off I had been dealing with after that. I could not trust anyone. Nobody had known who the guy was or why he had done that, it had been beyond my understanding at that point. I was pissed off. I went on a personal war path. I had not found out until I was transferred to another prison that Turtle's brother was the one who did that to me. He made it home and I heard he got shot. I've never known if he died. I would not have been mad if he did. I earned that scar through arrogance.

I had overlooked who I perceived to be weak and harmless. I would never make that mistake again. I would over look no one, and I would never be in the yard watching TV or doing anything else that unconsciously again. I returned to my hypervigilant ways. In the streets I had been hypervigilant and watched everything. I do not know why I thought I could stop being that way even for a second. The same rules I played by in the street, I needed to use here. The same deception, ruthlessness, and intelligence that had kept me safe in the streets would keep me protected here as well.

I had cut, stabbed, and brutally beat several men over the years after that, for many different reasons. Some had been sneak thieves, meaning they would go into cells when they thought no one was watching, and take things that did not belong to them. In prison someone was always watching, being hypervigilant. I had not tolerated stealing. A situation happened where I had gone into a thief's cell and beat him so badly, he died two days later of unsustainable head trauma. He had gone to an officer and told them that he had slipped and hit his head on the sink. He went to the clinic and never came back. He died over two packs of cigarettes. He entered my cell and took them off the locker that I had left them sitting on. I would have given them to him, had he just asked me. I did not even smoke, I won them in a bet.

Others I had to be violent with happened because they tried to bogard the phones, weights, and tables in the yard. Some had been disrespectful like it could not happen to them. In prison at times it had not mattered how tough you were, there would always be someone else who felt tough enough to test you. Another reason I had to be violent at times was for gangbanging. We would extort dudes for drugs if they were getting them, we wanted in, some of us sold it for commissary. I did not get high, but the rest of the guys would smoke it up. It never sat well with me that you could smoke something that smelled like a**, sometimes tasted like it. At other times we dealt with rivals. Most of the time we had rivals amongst ourselves. We had different crews within the same crew. Most of the time when a new guy came into the spot, he would not primarily be concerned about supposed-to-be rivals doing something to him. He would be worried about his own crew transgressing against him.

After a while I had been named an official leader in my crew. I was a high ranking general, an OG, a shot caller. That had made it easier for me to get one of the boys under me to be violent on my behalf. Prison had no real money to be made. Compared to the money I had made over the years in the drug game, selling here had not seemed worth my while. I had not had the patience for it. There had been too many petty dudes and problems that came with the territory.

So, there I was, an OG posted up in the prison yard with life. I had no real money but had my social status which I could not eat but was nice to have. I had heard nothing about my daughter. Shawnika was pregnant with her second child, and my parents were still strung out on coke and dope. I had gotten along well with everyone in my crew, however I could not say the same about the rest of the guys in it.

There had always been some sort of power struggle going on about things: such as who was the toughest, who could control the young boys in the yard, or the young boys not trying to hear any of the marching orders that their OG's gave them. It all seemed so petty to me. I refused to choose sides in my crew because they all respected me. I had love for all of them and we were all supposed to be together, but that had not been the case. Two of my close comrades had come to conflict over some prison politics.

They ended up attacking each other. Some of the other dudes in the crew chose sides. Thirty of them went to the box. I was disappointed, and we looked bad as a crew. When dudes joined the crew, we were taught about Huey P. Newton and the Black Panther Party, The Black Guerilla Family: Asada Shakur, George Jackson, David Hillard, Bunchie Carter, Bobby Seals, and any other Black Nationalists and Freedom Fighters; yet generally all we had done was promote more Black on Black violence. It seemed contradictive, better yet was. In the crew we had highly respected Whites and Latinos as leaders, so it had not been strictly a Black thing.

When I was shipped to Clinton Max from Greenhaven Max, I had come to another crossroads in my life. A dozen of us were shipped out of the HAV after a CO had been almost stabbed to death. Ceasar from the Bronx had enough of that oppressive disrespectful racist hillbilly CO and poked him up in G Block. Ceasar used to be with the crew but had fallen back from it. He would tell me all the time that he had not liked the direction we were going in. He would say to me, "the pigs are violating us all the time and we do nothing about it, but we are quick to jump on another brother." Even though he fell back from the crew, he and I were still tight and hung out. We still had each other's backs.

In life I had come to find out, you could be guilty by association. My association with Ceasar had been enough to get me up out of that spot. Even if that meant they had to trump up some charges, I amongst others had to go. Clinton Max was a dark and gothic prison to me. Mice had run freely on the galleries. The place had been filled to the brim with men and boys condemned to do life sentences. Many men had died there of old age, drug overdose, or murder. I would be as G'd up as I wanted to be, but I would never leave prison. It seemed this is how I would live out my days and die there as many before me had as well.

Jungle was a Jamaican I grew up with in Mt. Vernon. I remember when he came to America. He had lived with his grandmother and two older uncles. He had been a shy kid who had not spoken much. He and I traded Nintendo games and just hung out on the block with the rest of the kids. He was doing life with no parole for double homicide. He greeted me when I arrived at the place. He called my name as I entered the lower F housing unit. I turned and saw him standing on the steps outside of the block. I recognized him immediately. We shared joy at that moment. We had been shuffled into the block. He had just enough time to say to me he would meet me in the yard when I came out.

We walked the yard and talked about old times. We made the moments we remembered more luxuriously exotic than they really had been. Even the bad times in the streets seemed like good times compared to what we were engulfed in. We had not been doing anything uncommon though. Our type of talk could have been heard anywhere in the prison system. Somehow the poorest, most dangerous hoods, transformed into wonderful places to be, with the best-looking females. The times had become the greatest and somehow, we were the center of attraction, 'That N****.'

I admit it was a mild delusion that most of us suffered from in prison. Somehow, we neglected to remember all the pain and suffering that had helped us get to where we were at. We neglected the struggle and misery that clothed our community. He informed me that his grandmother had passed away. One of his uncles had been murdered and the other one had been on the run for a body. He had been in Clinton for seven years without a disciplinary infraction. He cooked food and sold bowls of it on the food court he had in the yard, for cigarettes. There had been between one hundred and one hundred fifty food courts that littered the massive hills of Clinton's yard. The hills had about a fifteen-story elevation which had been settled on a deep slope from top to bottom. You had to have been in good shape to walk up to the top of that mini mountain. If not, you were stuck in the valley of the racetrack round dirt yard, where the workout areas and phones had been.

The food courts measured four by four yards of land, had enough room to plant a small garden, had a picnic table, and had a three-foot-high metal drum styled single or double oven and grill. The courts were enclosed in deteriorated wooden picket fences, that had been numbered. The hills were dangerous with narrow twisting and turning pathways. The ability to escape or flee from anything was a problem.

I was on court 23-A when I reached another milestone in my bid. The old wooden fence of the adjacent court to my right crumbled under the weight of a man who had fallen through it trying to flee his attacker. He had hit the ground hard. The knife wielding assailant had straddled him. I had been sitting on top of the picnic table with my boots on the bench and watched as it unfolded. I was not startled or impressed by what I had seen. I had already seen it one too many times, however I had been alert, hypervigilant.

I had not seen either of their faces at first because they had hoods covering their heads. The attacker had poked wildly at the guy on his back, he was fighting for his life. I had just sat there watching as if I were ring side at the main event, until I noticed something. The guy on his back was Big B. He had gotten a grip of the knife holding man's wrist, which had stopped his stabbing for the moment. I sprung up and crossed the fence in less than two seconds. B and I had locked eyes as I assessed the situation. He had been bleeding badly out of his face, neck, and upper body. I had seen the wet blood soaking his hoody up. The look on his face said, "do not let me die here."

I pulled the hood off the head of the guy on top. I could not place him, but he had looked familiar. He smiled at me as if he knew me. I kicked him right in his smile and had taken control of him, his knife had become mine. He scrambled to his feet; Jungle had come out of nowhere and stabbed him in the back repeatedly. Two dudes had rushed Jungle, four or five rushed them. A few moments later about twenty CO's in riot gear had rushed us all. I ended up in unit fourteen, that is Clinton's box. Jungle had been exonerated, he was there so long they chalked it up to him being at the wrong place at the wrong time. They couldn't have seen him doing anything. Jungle's mans that had held him down received long term keep lock in E block. Big B was still in the outside hospital hanging on to his last breath. June the guy who put B in the hospital, received a few stiches in his back, and then joined me in the box. He was one of my boys, we had been in the same gang as Big B.

He stabbed B up over a pair of Timberland Boots and a gold chain, that he claimed one of the boys had left for him with B before he went home from Auburn, when they had been there together, but never had given them to him. B had just pulled up to the spot and that had been his first day in the yard. June had been on long term keep lock in E block, that was why I had not met him formally. He said we had met in transit a few years back, when I had been on my way to Upstate Box and he was leaving there.

He had apologized, he thought the boys had put

me on to what was about to go down. The truth was they all knew I had not supported that type of nonsense and would have stopped it. I had not understood why they would want to see that happen to one of their own. Now B had been laid up in the hospital dying over some hand me down Timbs and gold chain. I was disgusted. I was done with the boys. I had been working backwards, I sent letters to all my comrades in the crew and let them know my position. They had all attempted to get me to choose sides. That was ultimately what had brought me to my decision. There had been too many sides. There was absolutely no real unity, it only appeared to have been.

I had still been an OG who had built a solid reputation. I learned that your reputation in the street and reputation in prison were two different things. Just because you were tough in the street did not mean you would be tough behind the wall. You had some that were cowards behind the wall but would've killed you in the street. Then there had been those who were tough wherever they were at. Everyone had gotten tested, no one was exempt from that, whether it was mentally, physically, or both in some way.

My Realizations

I had decided to be consistent with my thoughts, ways, and actions. I had chosen not to be contradictive with them. The way I had previously chosen to live my life and view things were contradictive, inconsistent, and way too illogical. For instance, I would be upset when I heard about police killing unarmed Black men, women, and children. However, I still would not hesitate to kill another Black male myself.

Example: If Police murdered Tyheem I would be mad, but if I killed Tyheem's brother over some nonsense I'd be fine with it.

That was considered inconsistent, contradictive thought and action. I had to place as much value on a Black life as I had expected a police officer or any other group of people to do. I realized Black lives mattered to me, just as all lives did in general. I could not expect other ethnic groups to appreciate my beautiful Black people, if I myself did not. I had realized that when I carried guns and sought violence I did so for other Black males like myself. I did not carry guns for White people, Chinese people, Latinos or even the police. I held my wrath mainly for other Black folks. Clergy members such as Preachers, Reverends, Ministers, Priests, Popes and Imams have tried to use religion as a tool to calm violence, but it continues at an uncontrollable level. More prisons have been built and more males and females have been given life sentences to die in them.

The scared straight programs for youth are not really scaring them straight. I used to watch them when I was in Sing Sing on the "flats". They would be shuffled past our cells with a Correction Officer and some chosen model inmates that would explain prison and prison life to the kids. The kids never seemed afraid. It was as if many of them were searching for a loved one. As if they would discover their father, uncle, grandpa, cousin, brother, or family friend in one of the many cells they passed by. Maybe a few of the young white kids were nervous, but the Black and Latino kids wore their trip to Sing Sing like a badge of honor. They walked down the gallery with diddy bops, smirks, and ice grills on their young faces.

I doubt that any of them could grasp what we were experiencing on their quick overwhelming tour of the prison. Our pain was more psychological than apparent. It was not like the movies would portray prison with frantically screaming mad men glued to the cell bars yelling at them, spitting at them, and trying to grab them as they passed by. We carried on quietly with our sentences as they carried on quietly with their tour, that was that. There were times I would be ashamed to be seen by them and there were times that I would face them and see the same shame in their faces. They were my young people. I loved them and felt sad for them, and they did not even know it. Many of them had been court mandated to come in as a last attempt to keep them out of jail. They were already caught up in the system.

Behind the wall the vast majority of little homies and homies in general were disinterested in hearing somebody preach to them about what they should and should not be doing. They were more interested in getting high, getting a female, getting some money, getting home, or getting a knife or razor. For the most part outside of that you were wasting your words regarding the right and wrong way for them to live. I felt that way too, I didn't want to hear any preaching. We were all caught in the cycle at different stages.

If you didn't have a G.E.D. or needed Adult

Basic Education, most prisons would make it mandatory that you would be put in school for one of them. The irony of that was many guys refused to go to school. If they did go many would applaud, yell, and cheer when they found out that their class would be closed. The same rang true for vocational classes: custodial maintenance, plumbing, electrician, welding, computer repair, and carpentry classes; to name a few. Two hundred years ago it was illegal for Black Americans (who were then slaves) to have any type of education. It was against the law for them to know how to read, write, or count. Now that it had been legalized, many of us did not want it, even hated it. They would rather be kept locked in their cell, or in the box, than to learn to read and write. Whenever I heard joyful heckles and clapping because school would be closed, I felt disappointed, because I had a deep respect for education and understood its importance and power. I realized that a formal education meant nothing to many men. They felt all they needed to be was street smart, because that is where they had lived and survived. If they were ever to return to the street, that is where they would be until they died. That was street life and street life mentality. I must admit even though I felt this way about education I made no attempts to enroll in school either, because I was too busy doing nothing. It seemed that many of the old school shot callers had degenerated to shucking and jiving for showers on the gallery or a porter spot to sweep up and mop the prison floors. Many were blatantly disrespected daily and did nothing about it. All the glorified jail stories I had heard about as a boy along with the pictures I had seen of big men with jewelry on and the beautiful women who went to see them; only had a small piece of the truth, the rest were all lies.

I watched a man with a life sentence cry because his 19-year-old son had just received 25 years to life for murder, and there was nothing he could do for him. He had been in prison for his son's entire life. He had always projected an image of strength to his son from behind the wall. His son idolized the hood legend of his father and the perception of power that others claimed his father had behind the wall. Pistol knew his son would have to learn the hard way with at least 25 years of his life in prison, if he made it that far. His son Lil P represented another generation lost to the prison system.

After that I thought about my own daughter who I had not seen in years. I wondered what she was like, and then I had a thought I had never had before; I wondered if any of the guys I had murdered over the years had children. I was ashamed and cried for them, because I realized that they no longer had a father. That was the first time that empathy had struck me at the core of my being. I dared not tell anyone about my personal revelation, because in prison that could be interpreted as a weakness. In prison a weakness could be preyed upon, at least that was my thought process at the time. It was silly for me to think that way, because Pistol had cried in front of me, and I did not look at him as any less of a man. I and many men knew that there was nothing weak about him. I had to re-evaluate and question myself. Was I being too hard?

I was sad inside on too many levels to count. My life consisted of countless bad decisions, one after another for as long as I could remember. I wanted to reverse and do the right thing in life, however at that point I did not see it as a credible option. I had done too much and gone too far. One thing for certain is that I wish I had realized and understood the power of my decisions early on in life. I never thought about any long-term consequences and the effect they could have on myself or others, in that sense I had been selfish. The wrong choices can cost one dearly. Many say that it is alright to make mistakes. If a mistake causes a person their life, then mistakes are not alright because no one can resurrect the deceased, nor stop the lengthy prison sentences for murder, drug trafficking, or other. In the court of law ignorance is not a defense, you still must pay for the crime whether you knew it was a crime or not. It did not matter if I was ignorant, stupid, or illogical my whole life or part of it, I had to wake up!

DeShawn Kenner

Reversal

After I had been released from the SHU, I was transferred to Five Points Maximum Correctional Facility in Romulus, NY. Five Points is a Supermax with cameras everywhere. Something fantastic happened for me while I was in Five Points. I had been granted a full reversal on my case. I would be going back to court for a new trial.

Although I had turned myself in, I never pled guilty to the crimes I had been charged with. I had stood trial. My conviction was overturned for two reasons. One was that a juror said she could not be fair and impartial, if she knew that I had killed a person for any reason. Even though the juror could not be impartial which was a requirement of a potential juror, she went on to become one of my twelve jurors. Second, I had been charged with two counts of murder. They were intentional murder and depraved indifference murder. Legally I should've only had one count of murder on my indictment, not two. Intentional murder meant that I had planned to do it and depraved indifference meant that the act I committed had been reckless enough to cause murder. It was like going to the zoo and opening the lions cage. With either charge you would be facing twenty-five to life. The only difference was the wording.

I had learned over the years from when I went to the law library, that the law was just a word game. One big play on words and word semantics. What you had to say was important, however how you stated it and then wrote it was even more important. Your freedom would depend on it, complimented by facts and other theories. In the streets when a Black man knows how to put words together and express himself, he would be considered a slick talker, con man, or pimp. It seemed to me that slick talkers also wrote the law. For instance, in the Constitution where it states a Black man is a man, but only three-fifths of a man not a whole man. That to me was some real articulated slick talking that took place over two hundred years ago.

I shared the great news of my reversal with my bunky. That was the guy I lived in the cell with. Five Points was a double bunked prison. There were two males to a cell, with bunk beds. I landed in the cell with a comrade, a guy I didn't have to worry about. We shared the same values. We were both no nonsense, no homo, all the way men, and remain that way. I am briefly going to say something about homosexuality behind the wall.

I do not know about other states but in New York max prisons, men nor boys 99.9% of the time were not subjected to being raped. Maybe in times past, but not now. It was not tolerated by the general prison population. The guys who were known to be gay stayed in their own group. The guys who called themselves creeping on the low with a homosexual, when found out were dealt with. Some lost all their heterosexual friends and others were cut or stabbed depending on what group they had belonged. Being gay was not a label, that men or boys in prison wanted to have. When I had watched prison-based shows on television it seemed as if homosexual activity and rape were portrayed as a normal occurrence that most prisoners participated in, which is far from the truth. Being gay was either a choice or who the guy naturally was. It was not who I was or something I would ever choose to do. There are many men who feel the same way I do about the issue and it did not matter if they had life in prison. If they crossed the line, they were considered weak. They had let perverted, deviant lust take away their last piece of dignity a man could choose to hold onto behind the wall. Or I guess they had chosen gay pride. For the record I have nothing against gay men, being one just isn't me.

KB and I had talked about my reversal for hours in that cell. He also had a life sentence for homicide. He was Haitian and had been incarcerated since he was 17 years old for crimes, he swore to me he did not commit. He had been convicted in Queens and was going on his seventeenth year in prison. I had read his entire case. I am no lawyer; however, I did not read or see any evidence that convinced me of his guilt. I had also been around him long enough to know his character; I knew when he was lying to me and telling me the truth. I wholeheartedly believed and still believe that he was innocent of what he had been convicted of, meanwhile I had been guilty as sin of doing what I had just received a full reversal for. He did not have the money or legal team to prove his innocence, and all his appeals had been denied.

A reversal is when your conviction has been overturned. I no longer had a life sentence. I must admit, it seemed to both of us that life had a mind of her own, with her own agenda that would not be fair to all who lived her. I felt like he deserved that reversal more than I did, because I had made the decisions to pull the trigger all the times I had. I had sold drugs and robbed without any regard for the consequences. While in prison I had almost been killed and had killed a man recklessly, without repercussion. I had even tried gangbangin' for no good reason at all. I had to ask myself why I had been given that blessing. I am not a religious person however I do believe in a higher power. Whatever the reason, I needed to find answers to how I got to this point, why it all seemed okay at the time, and if there were ways to help prevent future generations from the same fate. Let's begin this mission of discovery together, shall we?

DeShawn Kenner

Part Three:

Journey Through

Answers

DeShawn Kenner

Premise

I had read a little bit about faiths. I read about Christianity, Islam, Judaism, The Nation of Islam, The Nations of Gods and Earths, Rastafarian, Santeria, Yoruba, Quakers, Hinduism, Confucianism, Buddhism, Shinto, and the Gnostics. I respected them all. They all had wisdom to live by. The common denominator they all sought was peace. At heart that was all I wanted too. I needed it deep in my soul and in every part of my life, because I had none. I only had stress and anxiety that I had coped with by having an 'I don't care about anything' emotionally disconnected attitude, or by being violent. Those two reactions were just my attempts to establish equilibrium within my mind and body. Deep down I just wanted to treat others how I wanted to be treated. I desired to treat people with love, empathy, respect, kindness, and compassion. I wanted to help them and not hurt them, and I wanted to be helped and not hurt. I needed to get close to the most-high. Knowing myself became the mission, because it is said that the more you understand yourself, the closer to God you will be. Through myself I would come close to God, which for me represented peace in every way. My goal was spiritual not religious.

Religion had too many rules, represented red tape, and it divided more than it has united people, to me. Most big wars in history were fought over religion. Even today those conflicts exist between Christianity, Islam, and Judaism; people still die for religion. The irony of that is religion is supposed to bring peace and unity, yet all I see it doing is causing war and division. If I did choose a religion and a religious crusade ensued, I would have to be willing to kill or die for it. I would be the same ole killer with a different cause. In my own eyes I wouldn't have changed at all.

I remember having been on Fordham Rd. in the Bronx shopping and stopping at an Army Recruiting Station on the bridge. One of the recruiters asked me to sign up and fight for my country. I signed up but did not have a High School Diploma or GED at the time to seal the deal. The Twin Towers had not yet been hit by the airplanes, on 9/11. If I had already had my GED I would have gone to war and been willing to kill for the honor of my country. Killing would still have been a requirement I had to be willing to do. It would have been considered a righteous cause to kill. In my eye, once again I would have not changed. Should I have rebuked murder or found a better cause to do it? Military personnel are regularly thanked for their patriotic service to their country. A part of that service may include murder, it coincides with protection. For the record, I support our troops, I am an American. I have loved ones who have served and those who continue to serve as I write these words.

It seemed to me that intention dictated whether killing was justified or not. The first murder in the Bible, Torah, and Koran is of Cain killing his brother Abel; over jealousy, envy, and greed. God looked upon that act unfavorably. In the same books' old testaments is the story of David and Goliath. David was the young Hebrew who killed the Philistine giant for his people. God looked upon this act favorably. No matter the intentions of it, killing has existed long before myself and others. Men considered both good and bad have committed this act. It appears to me that it will still be taking place for generations to come.

Violence

Violence is the world's most serious health problem. It maims and kills people daily. -World Health Organization

How does a person come to kill? Is it a sickness? Is it brainwashing or learned behavior? Is it solely based on survival, or is it man's nature? I cannot answer those questions with wholehearted clarity of the exact truth, however I can answer for myself. Simply put, murder had been my choice. I made the decision to pull the trigger or be violent when there was not a gun available.

I decided what clothes I would put on each day. I decided what I would eat or if I even would eat if I didn't like what was available to me. I chose to disrespect the teacher that had me expelled from school. I decided that I wanted a gun and that I would shoot it. I did not have to pick up a gun. There were many people I grew up with who chose not to, but I did. For me it was easy to do the wrong thing and difficult to do the right thing. Maybe poor neighborhoods were designed for the wrong thing to be easy to do. If I personally hadn't grown up in one would I have been less prone to violence?

According to the uniform crime reports published by the FBI in 1986 Blacks accounted for 46.6% of all arrests for violent crimes, even though Blacks comprised 12% of the US Population. Blacks accounted for 48% of the persons arrested for murder. Blacks accounted for 49.5% of all arrests for violent crimes: murder, forcible rape, robbery, and aggravated assaults. In 1986 Blacks under the age of 18 years old accounted for 54.9% of those arrested for violent crimes. The highest violent crime rates are demonstrated by young Black males.

More Black males died in one year, 1977,

than died in ten years in the Vietnam War. That was a year before I was born. The report goes on to say Black males are six times as likely as White males to be murder victims. Murder is the fourth leading cause of death for Black males. Ages 15 to 29 are the most dangerous years for Black males to die by murder. Most violent crimes 84% of which against Blacks were committed by Black offenders. Why had this become the case? In order to discover the reasons, I had to backtrack and find the common threads through human behaviors.

The adolescent time of my life was definitely the most dangerous era of my existence, because those were the days when I could not give trouble a rest. I would always be involved in some type of risk, even if there had been no reward to gain. Apparently, I was not alone, because adolescence is the most crime prone time all over the world (Dicanio, 1993 and Karger,

2014).

The adolescent age ranges from 12-25 years old and is described by Webster's New World Dictionary as "the time of life between puberty and maturity." Some scientists have considered adolescence to start as early as 10 years old and end at 30 years old when sampling the group for study (Wiley, 2017). Children between the ages of 13 through 24 in America account for 48.5% of the nation's homicide arrest, and 52% of the violent crime arrest (Dicanio, 1993). Scientific study of crime revealed that for decades crime has been clustered in certain neighborhoods (Dicanio, 1993). According to The New Jim Crow by Michelle Alexander, "the hyper segregation of the "Black-poor" in ghetto communities has made the round up easy; confined to ghetto areas and lacking political power the "Black-poor" are convenient targets." (Alexander, 2012).

My question then is, what happens when the poison of despair completely consumes the entire body of an environment, and affects the perception of the youth in the **biological ecological system** regarding adolescent development? The question is important because economically challenged crime and drug infested communities (red-zones) are at such high toxic levels of desperation; that many of their young residents are running the risk of becoming endangered species, if they are not considered so already. Solutions are urgently needed and the ultimate goal of the question I asked. The goal is no easy task; however, something can be done. The keys to intervention can be made to save our at-risk adolescents by examining their 1) **environment,** also by reprogramming their 2) **reaction to rejection,** and by actively attending to their 3) **mental health.**

Psychologist Urie Bronfenbrenner argues

that in order to understand human development one must consider the entire *ecological system* in which growth occurs **(Bronfenbrenner, 1994).** His system is composed of five socially organized subsystems that help support and guide human growth. They range from the **microsystem**, which refers to the relationship between a developing person and the immediate environment such as family and school. The next is the **mesosystem**, which has interaction between the family, teachers, the child's peers, and the neighborhood. Followed by the **exosystem** which involves links between a social setting in which the individual does not have any active role in the individuals' immediate context. For example, a parent's or child's experience at home may be influenced by the other parent's experience at work. The parent might receive a promotion that requires more travel which might increase conflict with the other parent and change patterns of interaction with the child. The **macrosystem** describes the culture in which individuals live. Cultural context includes developing and industrialized countries, socio-economic status, poverty, and ethnicity. The last subsystem is the **chronosystem** which is the patterning of environmental events and transitions over the life, as well as sociohistorical circumstances. Divorces are transitions in which researchers have found the negative effects of divorce on children often peak in the first year after the divorce on children. By two years after the divorce family interaction is less chaotic and more stable. An example of socio-historical circumstances is the increase in opportunities for women to pursue a career during the last thirty years (Bronfenbrenner, 1994). As well as the effects of legalization of reading, writing, and formal education for African Americans in the last 160 years. It represents the journey from total illiteracy to becoming educated people such as; Biologist Ernest Everett Just, Lawyer Thurgood Marshall, Mathematician Katherine Coleman or President Barack Obama.

Bronfenbrenner's model is well said and easy to understand, for that reason I will use it as a guide to find the flaws of perception development regarding adolescents in toxic environments. At the **microsystem** level many families of at-risk youth are excessively poor and supported by a single parent. In Black communities many men are missing from the household. Thousands of Black men have disappeared into prisons and jails, locked away for drug crimes that are largely ignored when committed by Whites (Alexander, 2012). The inference being that institutionalized racism may play a part in the dysfunctional **microsystem** which directly affects a child's perception developing in it. The mass incarceration of people of color is a big part of the reason that a Black child born today is less likely to be raised by both parents than a Black child born during slavery (Alexander, 2012). This variable gravely affects the perception of the minority adolescent. Another factor that plays a significant role in the perception development of an adolescent at the **micro level** is child abuse. According to the American Association for Protecting Children, a division of the American Humane Society, reported 2.2 million cases of child abuse in 1988, the average age was seven. Scientists found that children experiencing physical abuse at home showed an excess of aggressive and violent behavior by the time they entered kindergarten, regardless of whether they came from a well to do or a poor family, lived in a one parent or two parent household, or regularly observed cooperative or physically violent behavior among adults (Dicanio, 1993).

Psychologist Karen Horney stressed the importance of early parent-child relationships in her theory of personality development (Hergenhahn and Olsen, 2007). Components of her theory insisted that the two basic needs in childhood are safety and satisfaction. If these needs are not met it is because of basic evil, which causes basic hostility, and basic anxiety in the child. (Hergenhahn and Olsen, 2007). Horney called the behavior of parents that undermines a child's security, the basic evil. Some examples of such behavior are: 1) indifference toward the child, 2) rejection of the child, and 3) hostility toward the child (Hergenhahn and Olsen, 2007). A child abused by the parents in one or more of the preceding ways experiences basic hostility toward his or her parents (Hergenhahn and Olsen, 2007). The feeling of hostility caused by the parents does not remain repressed. Instead it is generalized to the entire world and all the people in it. The child perceives everything and everyone as potentially dangerous because of this perception the child experiences basic anxiety (Hergenhahn and Olsen, 2007). Horney's view perceived that a child with basic anxiety is well on his way to becoming a neurotic adult (Hergenhahn and Olsen, 2007). Horney summarized a list of neurotic needs into three major adjustment patterns, each pattern described the neurotics adjustment to other people (Hergenhahn and Olsen, 2007). The three patterns of adjustment are: 1) moving toward, 2) against, 3) away from people (Hergenhahn and Olsen, 2007).

Horney theorized the child on the way to becoming a neurotic would adjust in one of three ways. First, the child would be excessively submissive and avoid confrontations at all costs. They become the ultimate pleasers. Second, they would become excessively hostile and aggressive. As if to say I will hurt everyone else before they have a chance to hurt me. Third, they would become extremely aloof. As if to say if I withdraw from everybody, nothing can hurt me. I wonder if I experienced basic evil during my childhood at the **microsystem** level. If so, which adjustment did I choose?

The dysfunction of the family spills over from the **microsystem** into the **mesosystem**. For the adolescent whose parent or parents have no connection with the child's teachers or friends, because of substance abuse, incarceration, extra-long hours at their job/s, their own mental health issues; or because of failing school and unconcerned, detached teachers. The youth's issues are further expanded into the **exosystem** by their guardians' economic statuses; ex: parent loses job because of lack of education, criminal record, or welfare program funding cuts. In a document they issued, "The Key National Policy Issues for 1978," the Congressional Black Caucus Legislative Agenda, stated the essential problems they isolated as requiring immediate attention were: the exceptionally high rate of unemployment which continues in the nation as a whole; the disproportionate jobless rate among minorities in particular the continuing discrimination against Black persons, and other minorities, and the continuing inadequacies in health, education, welfare, housing, social service, and many other aspects of a decent quality of life for all of the nation's citizens (Palley and Palley, 1981).

According to the "New Jim Crow," President Bill Clinton, more than any other president, created the racial under caste. He signed the Personal Responsibility Act, which ended welfare as we know it, replacing it with Aid to Families with Dependent Children (AFDC), with block grants to states called Temporary Assistance to Needy Children/Families (TANF). TANF imposed a five-year lifetime limit on welfare assistance, as well as permanent lifetime ban on eligibility for welfare and food stamps for anyone convicted of a felony drug offense, including simple possession of marijuana (Alexander,2012). The **exosystem** explains variables affecting the parent(s) or guardian(s) directly influencing the perception and behavior of the child well into adolescence and possibly beyond. Do you think I was affected by any of these variables throughout my life, if so how?

The deterioration of the adolescents' **exosystem** is spread into the **macrosystem** where other adolescents share the same culture of poverty and parental absence throughout the community. Collectively the perception of this disenfranchised demographic becomes clear that they belong to the rejected class of society. Their social status is easily identifiable throughout their community which further deteriorates the developing perception of the adolescent. According to criminologist, James W. Wilson's "Broken Window Syndrome Theory," the syndrome arises when unfixed broken windows, uncleared graffiti, overgrown weeded lots, and other signs of decay demoralize a neighborhood's residents. Petty disturbances such as loud radios and voices, frighten ordinary citizens out of proportion to their seriousness, and fear makes them shun the streets. The absence of responsible adults on the streets encourages a cycle of deterioration, additional fear, and more crime (Dicanio, 1993). The youth are subject to become the victims of the caused circumstances and at the same time become the perpetrators of its negative cyclical affects. The broken window syndrome has spread beyond deteriorating neighborhoods and might be described as the, "abdication of responsibility through fear syndrome (Dicanio, 1993)". "Where once a youngster sitting on a bus picking the chocolate off his ice cream bar and dropping it on the floor would have been reprimanded by an adult; the behavior is now ignored because the child may well have a gun or a knife in his pocket. Violence has become common place, no one wants to die over slivers of chocolate underfoot (Dicanio, 1993)."

The government has been the main perception altering vehicle in the **bio-ecosystem** of the minority poor, starting at their youngest ages. Douglas Massey and Nancy Denton's book "American Apartheid" documents how racially segregated ghettos were deliberately created by federal policy, not impersonal market forces or private housing choices. The enduring racial isolation of the ghetto poor has made them uniquely vulnerable in the war on drugs

(Alexander, 2012). "Federalism" the division of power between the states and the federal government – was the device employed to protect the institution of slavery, and the political power of slave holding states. Even the method for determining proportional representation in Congress and identifying the winner of a presidential election (the Electoral College) were specifically developed with the interest of slaveholders in mind (Alexander, 2012). Also, under the terms of the country's founding document, slaves were defined as three-fifths of a man, not a real man, whole human being, upon this racist fiction rest the entire structure of American democracy (Alexander, 2012). At the **chronosystem** level, generation after generation of troubled adolescents have lashed out over failing, or failed public policy, from the American Revolution to the civil rights movement. In many cases, they do not even realize where the root of their problems stem from. Adolescents as young as ten years old have been reported to law enforcement authorities for violent fights over the presidency of Donald Trump. An environmental climate of religious, racial, cultural friction, and division continue to actively shape the perception of the most vulnerable minds, those of our children. Ironically enough in a post, Obama World, this is happening. How children express themselves is unthinkable apart from their environment. It is useless and potentially misleading to try to separate the relevance of nature and nurture regarding the course of their adolescent development (Shonkoff and Phillips, 2002). Status, roles, norms, and rules shape the developing psychological perception throughout Bronfenbrenner's ecological model of human development, also sometimes called the **bio-ecosystem** theory, because a person's own biology may be considered as part of the

microsystem. Do you think my environment helped shape my perception and behavior? Another substance that remains consistent throughout an adverse **ecosystem** is **rejection**.

According to London, Downey, Bonica, and Paltin, being rejected by one's peers is a potent predictor of both current and future relational difficulties. Such difficulties include aggression, social anxiety, withdrawal, and loneliness (London, Downey, Bonica, and Paltin, 2007). As an adolescent, I as well as countless other young teen boys from different parts of the same ruined environment were at odds. At some point we seemed to have become nurtured enemies, because we were from different blocks or buildings. Those petty differences kept the sense of rejection fresh in our minds. I would lash out violently or withdraw from those who made me feel like an outsider. Girls in my neighborhood were on the same page as well, rejection struck us all. We all hated police the same, because they seemed to disrespect and humiliate us every chance they could. There is no evidence of gender difference in the level of angry expectations of rejections (et al, Downey, 1998). An **ecosystem** that cycles rampant rejection creates the expectation of it in its' young minds. Experience of rejection whether active or passive, can sensitize children to the possibility of rejection (Downey, et al, 1998). This sensitivity takes the form of expectations of rejection that become activated in situations where rejection is possible and are accompanied by "hot" or defensive emotional states- anxiety or anger; that prepare the child to defend the self against subsequent rejection (London, Downey, Bonica, Paltin, 2007).

Intervention is possible because social acceptance techniques may reverse rejection sensitivity affects. An experimental intervention in which Robiner and Coie (1989) found that peer rejected girls who were led to expect acceptance from a new peer group were better liked by that peer group than a control group of peer rejected girls (London, Downey, Bonica, Paltin 2007). Also, experimental studies of children's ability to delay immediate gratification indicate that attentional cooling strategies help dampen frustrated arousal inherent in delay task, enabling resistance to temptation, and effective regulation of appetitive impulses (Ayduk, Mischel, & Downey, 2002). Correlation studies suggest that the cooling mechanisms that are critical of self-regulation in the delay-of-gratification task may also protect individuals who defensively expect and intensely react to rejection from maladjusted outcomes as aggression and low self-esteem (Ayduk, Mischel, & Downey, 2002). Also, the role of delay ability was examined in the context of rejection sensitivity (Downey and Felman, 1996). Childhood delay ability buffered both adults and pre-adolescents high in "rejection sensitivity" against aggression, low self-esteem, and interpersonal difficulties (Ayduk, Mischel, & Downey, 2002). A cross sectional study of pre-adolescent boys at-risk for aggression showed that the spontaneous use of cooling strategies in delay task (ex. looking away from the rewards and self-destruction) predicted reduced verbal and physical aggression (Ayduk, Mischel, & Downey, 2002). Development and cognitive research point at similar attentional processes in regulating negative behavior (Ayduk, Mischel, & Downey, 2002). For example, eye gaze aversion, flexible attention shifting, attention focus, and resistance to attentional interference are related to reduced impulsivity and anger even in early childhood (Ayduk, Mischel, & Downey, 2002).

Scientist-psychologist Albert Bandura (1973)

observed that children whose parents employed considerable corporal punishment often became highly aggressive, such children also tend to be less obedient (Hergenhahn and Olson, 2007). Bandura supports neither the extensive use of corporal punishment nor "unconditional love," because he believes that unconditional love is self-defeating, because it eliminates the informative relationship between performance and reward; in the absence of this relationship children are directionless (Hergenhahn and Olson, 2007). Also Bandura (1977) in accordance with his version of social learning theory emphasizes modeling, also known as imitation or observational learning, as a powerful source of development. For example: the baby who claps his hands after his mother does so, the child who angrily hits a playmate in the same way he has been punished at home, and the teenager that wears the same clothes and hairstyle as her friends at school; are all displaying observational learning. (Berk, 2008.) Youth must be taught positive productive ways to deal with rejection through rejection sensitivity intervention, self-control, delayed gratification techniques, and performance and rewards strategies. This ensures they will make the best decisions for themselves and their communities to grow in a more successfully developing mature manner and not a self-defeating one. I will now turn to the issue of mental health.

Mental health issues have erupted and spilled into every inch of a failed **bio-ecosystem**. Adolescents are most affected by the damage, because they end up in trouble the most already (Dicanio, 1993). PTSD (Post traumatic stress disorder) affects children especially those who have been victims of abuse or have lost a loved one (Dicanio, 1993). PTSD and Schizophrenia often go untreated in impoverished areas and

Schizophrenia usually occurs during adolescence or early adulthood (Dicanio, 1993).

The most common type of Schizophrenia that is associated with violence is the "paranoid type" (Dicanio, 1993). Paranoid Schizophrenics are often characterized by unfocused anxiety, anger, argumentativeness, and violence (Dicanio, 1993). They interpret the actions of others as deliberately demanding or threatening in at least four ways: 1) he or she expects without sufficient evidence to be exploited or harmed by others; 2) he or she is easily slighted and quick to anger or counter attack; 3) he or she bears grudges or is unforgiving to insults or slights; 4) he or she is reluctant to confide in others because of unwarranted fear that the information will be used against him or her (Dicanio, 1993). Mood disorders are defined by the DSM-III-R as having as an essential feature, a disturbance of mood, accompanied by a full or partial manic, or depressive syndrome that is not attributed to any other mental or physical disorders. Mood disorders are divided into bi-polar and depressive disorders.

ADHD (Attention Deficit Hyperactivity Disorder) is another issue. ADHD can lead to emotional or behavioral problems, difficulty with peer relationships, and difficulty within the family. Unrecognized and untreated the disorder will interfere greatly with all aspects of the child's or adolescent's life (Silver, 1993). Adolescence is a time to be mentally monitored, because around the world adolescence is a time of heightened sensation seeking and immature self-regulation (Wiley, 2017). Many neurological developmental issues have yet to be answered. Our youth need observation and guidance, because many mental health problems have not yet been solved for them. Mental health help and continued investigation is a must for our at-risk adolescent class or caste. Many of our mentally ill youth end up in prison where their mental health issues are further disregarded, and in many cases, made worse.

Countless criminologists, behavioral scientists, and sociologists have reasoned that drug addiction, lack of education, capitalism, learning disabilities, lack of job skills, unemployment, government laws, and Black male irresponsibility to name a few have been the leading causes of Black criminality and Black on Black violence. Could my life's outcome have been created and predicted before I was even thought about? Or did I just play into the easiest available options? I think back on my predecessors like Powerful and Speedy, and with the ease that they gave me guns to protect myself with. Also, drugs to sell so that I could have money to eat with, buy clothes with, and over all just so I could survive.

Maybe they had known something I did not know and just did not know how to tell me at my young age. They had come up and were in power in the streets during the 80's and I was coming up in the 90's. Maybe they already knew that the streets were a dangerous and hungry place for Black males and that there would be no jobs available for me. Maybe they already knew that the police were not there to serve and protect me, and I would instead have to protect myself. Vigilant justice had been the dominant justice in poor Black neighborhoods all throughout America. I was young, I had guns, and I took matters into my own hands. I became a vigilant vigilante. Street law had become my law, and I never looked back or questioned it.

Positive, productive, forward moving progress can be made for at-risk adolescents by **investigating their environment**, by **reprogramming their rejection reaction**, and by **making sure that their mental health needs are met**. It is not an easy task, but our future relatives will have a cleaner **ecosystem** in which they can raise children with untainted – positive, pure, perceptions of themselves, others, and the world we all live in; or at least the world they will all be living in.

Solution

This is based on the Author's 'Formula Theory of Human Behavior' see in Appendix.

In order to create positive forward moving communities and powerful knowledge of self, and self-control; I now introduce to you The Loyalty Project. I have always been loyal to a fault, now I want to be loyal for the greater good and be sure all our youth learn to as well. The only way to change the outcome is by changing the path that leads there. This project addresses the main concerns outlined in the previous studies and reports.

The Loyalty Project is to help learn to become loyal for the good of yourself and your community. This program is to be integrated into all schools K-12 and to work hand in hand with required curriculum. This not only holds students accountable, but will also create a new accountability for teachers. In general, it should create a very harmonious school environment as well as community.

The primary purpose is to curb aggressive behavior in children and adolescents. As well as to teach all cultural backgrounds, religions based on history, and a full accurate world history; creating a better understanding of each other and limit assumed judgments. All programs will grow with them, from the point they are introduced, throughout their academic career and evolve continuing to handle all these issues at each advanced level.

The Loyalty Project:

Kindergarten

Self-Control simple consequence system with a three-warning system, reset with new start after lunch, and always encouraged to say how they could've avoided the consequence.

Delayed Gratification staying focused on the task at hand, knowing that the reward for following rules and doing necessary things; results in free time to do what they want to do.

Self Sufficiency being able to do all the following themselves: tie shoes, brush teeth, wash hands, clean face, take care of their belongings, and good treatment of self and others.

1st Grade

Role Playing problem solving with others and themselves.

Manners and Respect exhibiting these always while in the school community and carrying them into the community at large.

Growth Mindset allow students to fix homework/test mistakes and model real life application of it.

2nd & 3rd Grades

Preventing peer pressure, picking on others based on differences or perceived differences, desire to fit in, intro to time management and aggressive management strategies. Show short movies addressing these topics, reading level books should also cover these topics, and teach ways to handle conflict resolution well.

4th & 5th Grades

Community Involvement help at after school program, help prepare food, serve food, homework help for younger kids, etc.; adopt a grandparent from local nursing homes.

Group Problem Solving physical activities to create trust and working as a team to solve problems. Peer Review committee for problem solving and disciplinary measures.

Career Curriculum intro level create lists of likes/hobbies/interests, explore jobs, careers, and businesses that make these possible as adults.

Social Media reality vs perceived reality, self-love, staying away from comparing yourself with others, positive uses, and behavior.

6th, 7th & 8th Grades

Community Service find them organizations they can volunteer at within fields they are interested in and solves a problem they personally wish they could change.

Career Curriculum will review all the different avenues available to work in their preferred job fields such as college, trade, internship, or military. The goal is to have it narrowed down to help their freshman guidance counselor set their curriculum up for long term goal success.

Interview/Job 8th graders will do mock job interviews, research places that hire 14yo and older, obtain working papers, and have companies come in to discuss expectations from places they could apply to.

High School

Aggressive Management Strategies curriculum teaching them to recognize body cues to becoming aggressive, tactics to deal with anger, and alternative responses to physical altercations.

HS Mentors Program be paired with elementary aged kids, make sure they get to afterschool program, home safely, talk about the endless possibilities of their future, and let the district know any concerns the school community can help with.

Voting understand why it matters, how to determine whose views you agree with, and assistance registering to vote when 18yrs old; whether a current or former student.

Help Closet free food pantry for weekends, clothes, school supplies, plus laundry facility at school to wash clothes, and early access to school if they need to clean up prior to school.

Car Program from when they first start working, help them save money to be able to buy their first car. Also create a grant program that they can win based on community involvement, academics, and actively promoting positive choices.

There is an African Proverb that says it takes a village to raise a child. That is true mostly because it's teaching the child the importance of the respect and care for that village and the people in it. Once upon a time the purpose of school was to create good citizens, now we seem to be solely focused on testing, and schools that don't do well get less funding. The original red zone areas are the ones affected the most which is only perpetuating this viscous cycle. It is imperative all schools adopt The Loyalty Project; therefore, we will build a sense of a global community, respect for all people, and understanding of why we all must care for each other as one race, the human race.

Appendix

Formula Theory of Human Behavior "cycle" Individual Evolution

Step One:

Environment*Experience*Thought Process*Temperament=Perception

Step Two:

(Perception + Decision)*Behavior=Consequence

Step Three:

Cycle from Consequence back to Environment

Definitions of Formula Components:

1. **Environments** are the settings from which all

2. **Experiences** are formed through the five senses

3. **Thought Process** is the concentration and mechanism by which the brain can perceive concepts via neurotransmitters and the physical senses

4. **Temperament** is whether one has natural tendencies to be extroverted vs introverted, passive vs aggressive, or emotional vs stoic.

5. **Perception** is the outcome of the thought process, positive or negative

6. **Decision** choice based on the perception that one has of a situation

7. **Behavior** the decision acted out in the external environment

8. **Consequence** outcome of behavior acted upon stimulating positive or negative reinforcement of an action

References

Alexander, M. (2012). The New Jim Crow: Mass Incarceration in the Age of Colorblindness. New York: The New Press.

Ayduk, O., Mischel, W., and Downey, G. (2002). Attentional Mechanism Linking Rejection to Hostile Reactivity: The Role of "Hot" vs "Cool" Focus. Psychological Science, 13:433-448.

Berk, Laura E. (2008). Infants and Children, 6th Ed.

Bronfenbrenner, U. (1994). Ecological Models of Human Development. In International Encyclopedia of Education, 3:37-43. New York: Freeman.

Dicanio, M. (1993). The Encyclopedia of Violence: Origins, Attitudes, Consequences. New York: Facts on File.

Hergenhahn, B.R. and Olsen, M.H. (2007). An Introduction to Theories of Personality. Upper Saddle River, New Jersey: Pearson Prentice Hall.

Karger, S. and Basel, A.G. (2014). Teens Impulsively React Rather than Retreat from Threat. Developmental Neuroscience. 10.1159/000357755:1-8.

London B., Downey, G., Bonica, C., and Paltin, I. (2007). Social Causes and Consequences of Rejection Sensitivity. Journal of Research on Adolescence. 17 (3): 481-506.

Palley, M.L. and Palley, H.A. (1981). Urban America and Public Policies. Canada: D. C. Heath and Company.

Shankoff, J.P. and Phillips, D. A. (2000) From Neurons to Neighborhoods. Washington D.C.: National Academies Press.

Silver, L.B. (1993) Dr. Larry Silver's Advice to Parents on Attention-Deficit Hyperactivity Disorder. Washington D.C.: American Psychiatric Press Inc.

Webster's New World Dictionary (4th Ed) (2003) Cleveland: Wiley Publishing.

Wiley, J. (2016). Around the World, Adolescence is a time of Heightened Sensation Seeking and Immature-Self-Regulation. Developmental Science: Wileyonlinelibrary.com/journal/desc.

DeShawn Kenner

DeShawn Kenner

Suggested Reading

1. Drugs, Society, and Human Behavior by Dr. Carl L. Hart
2. Think Outside the Cell: An Entrepreneur's Guide for the Incarcerated and Formerly Incarcerated by Joseph Robinson
3. Mindset: The New Psychology of Success by Carol S. Dweck
4. The Color of Water: A Black Man's Tribute to His White Mother by James McBride
5. The Story of Christianity by Justo L. Gonzalez
6. Standing at The Scratch Line: A Novel (Strivers Row) by Guy Johnson
7. Technology of Teaching by B.F. Skinner
8. Destruction of Black Civilization: Great Issues of Race from 4500 B.C. to 2000 A.D. by Chancellor Williams
9. Breaking the Chains of Psychological Slavery by Na'im Akbar
10. Makes Me Wanna Holler: A Young Black Man in America by Nathan McCall
11. Between the World and Me by Ta-Nehisi Coates
12. The Bluest Eye by Toni Morrison

13. I Know Why the Caged Bird Sings by Maya Angelou
14. The Republic by Plato
15. The Audacity of Hope: Thoughts on Reclaiming the American Dream by Barack Obama
16. Letters to a Young Brother: Manifest Your Destiny by Hil Harper
17. Economic Logic by Mark Skousen
18. Classics in Social and Behavioral Sciences by Adam J. Heurle, PhD. & Robert C. Tash, PhD.
19. Guns, Germs, and Steel: The Fates of Human Societies by Jared Diamond, PhD.
20. Convicted in the Womb: One Man's Journey from Prisoner to Peacemaker by Carl Upchurch
21. The Way They Learn by Cynthia Ulrich Tobias
22. The Scourge of Racial Bias in New York States' Prisons NYT by Michael Schwirtz, Michael Winerip & Robert Gebeloff
23. Shook One: Anxiety Playing Tricks on Me by Charlamange Tha God

DeShawn Kenner

About the Author

DeShawn Kenner was born in Mount Vernon New York 1978. He was a hard-headed youth who took to the streets. He made many mistakes along his life's journey and hindsight is always 20/20. The author has been on a journey of self-discovery all his life. He has traveled through life's highs and lows in search of self. Through that time DeShawn wrote No More Mistakes Guide to Making Better Decisions, a book now widely used by Guidance Counselors for youth at a crossroads. Through DeShawn's next phase of self-reflection, he wrote Twelve Paths to Power the Art of Mastering Self, an introspective roadmap used by life coaches to help their clients peel back the layers and deal with core issues. While working on his Behavioral Science Degree through Mercy College and obtaining his Associates Summa Cum Laude, he has delivered us this current Masterpiece.

DeShawn Kenner